IN EARLY JUNE 1964,

the Benevolent Home for Necessitous Girls burns to the ground, and its vulnerable residents are thrust out into the world. The orphans, who know no other home, find their lives changed in an instant. Arrangements are made for the youngest residents, but the seven oldest girls are sent on their way with little more than a clue or two to their pasts and the hope of learning about the families they have never known. On their own for the first time in their lives, they are about to experience the world in ways they never imagined...

Small Bones

VICKI GRANT

ORCA BOOK PUBLISHERS

Library and Archives Canada Cataloguing in Publication

Grant, Vicki, author
Small bones / Vicki Grant.
(Secrets)

Issued in print, electronic and audio disc formats.
ISBN 978-1-4598-0653-5 (pbk.).—ISBN 978-1-4598-0656-6 (pdf).—
ISBN 978-1-4598-0655-9 (epub).—ISBN 978-1-4598-1098-3 (audio disc)

I. Title. II. Series: Secrets (Victoria, B.C.)
PS8613.R367S63 2015   jc813'.6   C2015-901744-0
C2015-901745-9
C2015-901746-7

First published in the United States, 2015
Library of Congress Control Number: 2015935519

Summary: In this YA novel, Dot enlists the aid of a local boy in her search for clues
about the parents who abandoned her as a newborn.

*Orca Book Publishers is dedicated to preserving the environment and has
printed this book on Forest Stewardship Council® certified paper.*

Orca Book Publishers gratefully acknowledges the support for its publishing
programs provided by the following agencies: the Government of Canada through
the Canada Book Fund and the Canada Council for the Arts, and the Province of British
Columbia through the BC Arts Council and the Book Publishing Tax Credit.

Cover design by Teresa Bubela
Front cover images by iStockphoto.com and Dreamstime.com;
back cover images by Shutterstock.com —
Author photo by Megan Tansey Whitton

ORCA BOOK PUBLISHERS
www.orcabook.com

Printed and bound in Canada.

18 17 16 15 • 4 3 2 1

This is for Flight Lieutenant R.B. Grant, DFC, and the many brave and foolish young men like him.

Raise your glasses high, boys.
Raise your glasses high.
Here's to the dead already
And here's to the next to die.

Prologue

July 9, 1947—Sometime after midnight

IT WAS DARK and he didn't know where he was going. He pulled over to check the map she'd drawn for him, but a lot of good that did. She hadn't been there in years. She'd scribbled vague lines on the back of a soup label and said, "The turn is right before the gas station, or maybe right after," then she'd drawn a long squiggle and, at the edge of the label, a box with a roof on it.

She'd pushed the paper across the kitchen table and said, "You'll find it. Not much else around there. Whole reason I left." Then she'd rubbed a smudge of blood off her hand and creaked to her feet. She didn't have time for this. She had her own pressing matters to attend to.

He chucked the map out the car window and got back on the road, gravel machine-gunning the bushes. He'd keep heading east.

A deer materialized in front of him, its eyes flat and shiny as new dimes. The man swerved but didn't slow down. He had to be back before dawn.

He was angry with her but knew he had no right to be. An old woman could hardly be expected to drive three hours along deserted back roads. Likewise, he certainly couldn't be left to deal with—he struggled for the words—*female issues*. So he had to drive. She had to take care of the rest. Simple as that. He'd been through worse.

His headlights stuttered over the potholes. He hadn't passed a car or a house in what seemed like hours. Even so, he found himself worrying that someone might happen upon the crumpled map at the side of the road and use it as evidence against him. He gripped the steering wheel and drove faster, his neck jutting toward the dashboard, a cartoon drawing of a guilty man on the run.

He was being ridiculous. Guilty? He leaned back, loosened his tie and took his first real breath in miles. He hadn't done anything wrong.

It was that damn girl. This was her fault. What had she been thinking? Or had she been thinking at all? That was the problem with kids today. They didn't think. They had it soft. Too many cheap novels and silly movies filling their heads with romantic crap. Love conquers all? That certainly hadn't been his experience.

She wasn't a child, for God's sake. She was seventeen. Old enough to know better. Well, she was paying for her foolishness now, wasn't she? He took off his hat and threw it in the backseat. Two families, two fine old families, could be ruined by this.

"Damn girl." He said it out loud this time. "Damn bloody girl."

It was just a turn of phrase, an affectation he'd picked up in England, but it made a picture pop into his head. He saw the white shirt soaked red with blood. The gray face. The crazy eyes. His anger melted into something closer to fear.

He reached across the passenger seat and pushed the edge of the towel away with his finger. The baby's face turned toward him. He jerked back in shock. He hadn't really expected it to be alive still.

There was a jar of milk on the car floor and a tiny spoon in his coat pocket. He was supposed to feed it if it got hungry. He didn't know the first thing about babies. Was it hungry?

It wasn't crying. It must be fine. That's what he told himself.

He stepped on the gas. What if he'd already passed the turnoff? What if the Mounties stopped him? How would he explain a newborn baby, especially one like this? Dinner napkin for a diaper, umbilical cord pinched off with a clothespin— they'd know there was something fishy. Who would he say it belonged to? What if it died? The questions wouldn't stop.

And then there, almost miraculously, was the gas station she'd mentioned, and just after that a road and, pointing the way, a sign half obscured by alders. Only the word *Benevolent* was legible. It gave him the creeps, that word, but he shook his head and carried on.

In minutes he was crawling up the long driveway. He pulled onto the lawn—he didn't want to get too close to the house—and killed the engine. He leaned his elbows on the steering wheel and rubbed his face in his hands.

Do it. Just be done with it.

He opened the car door, and the hinges shrieked. But no lights turned on, no dog barked, so he picked up the baby—small and alien as a newborn kitten, face like a rotten apple—and got going.

He wondered if he was doing the right thing. It wasn't too late. No one had seen him. The girl thought it was dead anyway. He could turn around, drive back down that deserted road, or another one just like it, and leave the baby somewhere no one would ever find it. It wouldn't survive long. Which was worse? A merciful death or a miserable life? It was a fair question and not the first time he'd had to ask it.

The baby squirmed. A tiny fist, gnarly as a wad of gum, jutted out from under the towel in some kind of salute. It's a tough little bugger, he thought. Then, despite himself, She's a tough little bugger. It's a she.

There was no going back now. He began picking his way across the lawn toward the Benevolent Home for Necessitous Girls. He realized that once upon a time, before the house had become an orphanage, someone grand must have lived here. The lord of the manor, no doubt, had had lots of foundlings left on his doorstep.

The thought shamed him. *A foundling. A common foundling.*

He turned around and got his old coat from the car. (She'd grabbed it from the hook by the door. Ran down the driveway after him. Insisted he take it.) It was July and would be sizzling by noon, but at three in the morning, it was cool and damp, and the baby was so horribly small.

He wrapped her in his coat, placed the bundle on the front step, then banged at the door until a lamp flicked on in a third-floor window. He was back on the road by the time he saw light flood across the verandah and a silhouette appear in the doorway. His shoulders relaxed. Someone will look after her, he thought. She's someone else's problem now.

He had three more hours before he'd be home. Plenty of time to think. More than he would have liked. He no longer had anything to distract him from the truth.

And the truth was this: The girl wasn't to blame. He was. He was the arrogant jerk who'd gotten this whole sorry thing started. He'd spend the rest of his life trying to figure out how to make it right.

One

June 1964
Just outside Hope, Ontario

THE BOY WAS LOOKING at me again.

I stood up to get something out of my suitcase. A baby laughed. I turned to see what was so funny and there he was, right behind a lady tickling her little girl. That's what I was really smiling at, but the boy must have thought I was smiling at him because he looked me straight in the eye and he winked.

A real wink. Not a there's-a-little-something-in-my-eye type of flutter or the full-fledged facial spasm of a homicidal maniac. This was a genuine hey-baby-how's-it-going wink.

It got me right in the spine. My legs buckled. I dissolved into my seat without getting whatever it was I wanted out of the suitcase. I didn't move again for ages, but inside my heart was clacking away like a Morse-code operator on a sinking ship. *Mayday. Mayday. Mayday.*

All I could think was, I wish Tess were here, or Toni or Cady. They'd know what to do. They wouldn't just sit there, staring at the greasy black bristles on the neck of the man in the row ahead. They'd look at the boy with their eyelids at half-mast and say, "I beg your pardon," and then they'd turn back to whatever they'd been doing and leave him there, blushing like a fool.

Unless, of course, he was cute, in which case they might go, "Take a picture, why don't you? It lasts longer." They'd say it with a smirk and a hand on one hip, and if he were worth bothering about at all, he'd understand it was an invitation to come back with an equally snappy remark. Make them laugh, and they might even let him talk to them for a while.

I wondered if the boy was cute.

I didn't know. He winked. I disintegrated. I barely saw him. A madras shirt. Blondish-brownish hair. Could have used a comb. Freckles.

There's no way I could have seen freckles from where I was. He was four rows back, and I'd only caught a glimpse of him. I must have been making up the freckles part.

I had to stop doing that.

Just a few days earlier, Mrs. Hazelton had taken my hand in both of hers and said, *Dot. Look at me. You have. To keep. Your wits about you. This is serious. No more flights of fancy. No more daydreaming. You're on your own now. I need you to promise me you'll do that.*

I turned away from the man's neck and looked out the window and tried not to cry. Fields, some with cows, slid past me. Barns I knew gave way to barns I'd never seen before; then they gave way to trees, trees and more trees.

It made me feel like Little Red Riding Hood. On my own, in the woods, wolves all over the place.

Every so often a cliff or a stand of fir blocked the sun, and then the train would go dark and the window would turn into a mirror, and I'd catch little flashing reflections of the lady behind me with the hat like a coconut layer cake or the lady with the baby or the boy.

His cheek was leaning against the window, and his arm was stretched out across the back of the empty seat beside him. His hair fell over his forehead as if he played in a band or something. He may have been asleep.

I realized he was indeed cute, and my heart went ape again.

And that brought me back to missing Sara and Toni and Malou and Betty and Tess and Cady and Joe the cook and the Little Ones and even Mrs. Hazelton, who I knew I drove to distraction but who up to this point had always managed to resist the urge to send me off into the woods alone.

I realized this was exactly what she meant by *flights of fancy*. I was hardly some kid in a cape, tripping through the forest with nothing to protect me but a basket of goodies. In a few weeks, I'd be seventeen. I was on a passenger train with comfortable seats and a bell I could ring for the conductor if I needed him. I had $127 in my brand-new purse. I had my very own suitcase, full of my very own clothes. I was wearing lipstick. A cute boy had winked at me.

A day earlier, all that would have sounded like one of my fantasies. I'd spent my entire life as a penniless, poorly dressed, unwinked-at orphan—and yet right now I'd have given it all up to go back to the Home. Suddenly, I had almost everything I'd ever dreamed of, but it didn't make me feel better. It made me feel like I needed to pee and/or throw up.

That probably sounds crazy. The average person hears the word *orphanage* and thinks gruel—or, in our case, lima-bean casserole—but it wasn't like that. I had a lot of happy memories. Bath nights. Holding the new babies. Lighting farts on fire. Toni killing herself as Mrs. Hazelton stood there tapping her foot while I tried to come up with some plausible explanation for the burn hole in the seat of my pants. Sara and I in the common room, doing the twist to the CHUM 150 hit parade long after everyone else had gone to bed.

There were some not-so-happy moments too, of course. Sharon falling down the cellar stairs with the potato peeler in her hand. Joe walking up the driveway with Puss 'n Boots in his arms, her neck at such a terrible angle that we didn't even have to ask. Patsy's grandmother showing up and taking her back. Marlene getting adopted, and Belinda getting adopted, and even Sharon getting adopted despite the scar.

The time I realized it was never going to happen to me.

The next stop was Firth. I could get off there and hop a train home. Malou might not have left yet. I could maybe even catch Sara.

That made me feel better until I remembered Mrs. Hazelton saying, *You can't. You can't stay here. There's nothing here for you.*

Even at the time, I knew she was right. The night before our little chat, I'd stood on the lawn, with Sara's arm around my shoulder and little Lindy sobbing all over my pajamas, and watched the fire rip through the Home.

By morning there was nothing left of our big white house but a charred black blotch. It was as if someone had tried to draw the place, then gotten mad because it didn't look right and scribbled the whole thing out with a giant Magic Marker.

I told Mrs. Hazelton it didn't matter. I could stay somewhere in town. I could work at the Welshes. I'd cleaned there three afternoons a week for the last two years and never had any trouble.

"No," Mrs. Hazelton said, like it was out of the question.

So I said I could work at Loretta's Diner or take in sewing. Mrs. Hazelton knew I was a good seamstress, but she just kept shaking her head, no matter what I came up with.

She'd let go of my hand. She said, "Dot... Dorothy..." and then I knew I didn't stand a chance.

"The people in Hope are decent—I'm not saying they aren't—but here's the hard truth. You stay in town, and you'll always be an orphan. Get a good job, marry a nice man, raise fine children—it won't make a whit of difference. You'll still just be a girl from the Home, and whether they mean to or not, they'll look down their noses at you." She put a smile on her face, but it was about the size and shape of a fingernail clipping so didn't offer much in the way of comfort. "Leave Hope and you can be whoever you want to be."

She made it sound so reasonable, so easy, but it wasn't, and it made me angry. All those years, any time a girl got adopted and I didn't, she told me I shouldn't be sad. I was the lucky one, she used to say. I was the one who got to stay at the Home with my friends—and now here she was, telling me I had to just ditch it all and get out.

"Where would I go?" I said, or more like screamed, but she didn't even flinch or say, *Watch your tone, young lady.* She just raised her eyebrows like, *Well, let's see…*

We were sitting in the study of her cottage, right behind where the Home used to be. There was a long, flat box on the desk between us. It was the type of box a dress would come in, but it was old and dusty, so I hadn't given it much thought.

Now she slid it closer and took off the lid. Whatever was inside stunk of mildew, but it was wrapped in tissue as if it was something precious.

She peeled open the paper and took out a man's over-coat. A large man's overcoat. Long. Beige. Double-breasted. Missing one button and half of another. She spread it on the desk, but it didn't want to lie flat. It was as if someone's elbows were still in the sleeves.

I felt like I was watching a magic trick or at least that part where the magician does stuff to distract you from what he's actually up to.

Mrs. Hazelton was up to something. She was throwing me out and trying to make it seem like she wasn't.

"Lovely, isn't it?" she said. I bit down on the inside of my cheek. No way I was letting her bamboozle me.

She flipped back the hem and looked at the label. "One hundred percent cashmere. Must have cost a pretty penny. Beautiful stitchery. You'll appreciate that."

She patted the hem back down, and then, without even looking at me, said, "This is what I found you in."

She let that sink in for a moment.

"Tiny, tiny little thing you were, wrapped up in this big coat. I almost didn't see you. Three in the morning. The verandah pitch-dark. For a second, I thought someone had just chosen an odd time to drop off some hand-me-downs."

My face went prickly from the inside out. Mrs. Hazelton had always just shaken her head when I'd asked her before, as if it was all some giant mystery. As if I'd just appeared at the Home one day out of thin air. Poof! A genuine magic trick.

The only reason I knew I was born too early was because I had to go to the doctor every year so he could listen to my heart. Once, he'd mentioned it was because I was premature, and for the longest time I thought that meant I hadn't started my period yet. (Toni straightened me out on that one. Nearly peed her pants laughing first, of course.)

Mrs. Hazelton unbuttoned the coat and laid it open. A big green stain more or less the shape of Africa had almost eaten through the lining.

"You had a little accident," she said, and I kind of blushed, although I don't know why. She could hold me accountable for a lot of things, but not that.

"I woke up Flossie Bradley—she was helping us out back then—and she ran for the doctor. I turned the stove on low and popped you in. Just like a loaf of bread on the rise. I'd heard they did that with the Dionne quintuplets, and I figured it was the only chance you had."

She held up her palm. "You were no bigger than this. Honestly. Like something you'd see in a jar at a traveling circus. Dr. Blunt came and just shook his head. No one thought you'd make it through the night. We dragged Reverend Messervey out of bed, and he had you baptized by dawn and ready to go. Flossie was the one who started calling you Dot. It was kind of a joke." Again that smile. "You were a little bigger than a dot, but not much."

Mrs. Hazelton was fiddling with the lapel of the coat now, trying to keep it from turning up at the edges. She was right about the stitching. The only time I'd ever seen hand-stitched lapels were on Mr. Welsh's suits. He owned the foundry, and everyone knew he was the richest man in town.

I had all sorts of questions, but my brain couldn't seem to turn them into words.

"You surprised us," she said, slapping the dust off her hands. "You survived. You even became a bit of a tourist attraction. People used to drive out here just to get a look at you. I thought you were going to be snapped up in no time, with those big eyes of yours. Then I realized these people were just sightseeing. Nobody wanted to take a chance on some problem cropping up down the line because of how little you were. One person—who will go nameless—even said he hoped you wouldn't grow to normal size. Said if we charged people to see you, we wouldn't have to rely on *charity* to keep the Home going."

She plumped up the back of her hair the way she did when she was outraged. "In any event, no one stepped up, so we got to keep you. And look at you. You turned out just fine."

"But now you want me to go." She shouldn't have reminded me.

"*Want*? No." Her lips turned down, and her nostrils got really big, and for one horrible second I thought she was going to cry, but then she said, "I almost forgot. There was something else too."

She reached into one of the coat pockets and pulled out a tiny spoon. A mustard spoon. I only knew what it was because I polished Mrs. Welsh's silver every Tuesday, and she was always very particular about her mustard spoons and her pickle forks and her fish knives and all the other fancy utensils only rich people seem to need to get their food into their mouths.

"It's sterling," Mrs. Hazelton said. "It was in the pocket, for some reason. Can you make out what the crest says? You've got young eyes."

I held the spoon up close and squinted at the handle. "I think it says *royal* or maybe *loyal* then…something something. *Loyal on the earth*?"

She nodded, but I wasn't sure if she meant "could be" or "doesn't matter."

The train suddenly juddered. A little girl screamed. The man in front of me held on to his hat like a cowboy on a bucking bronco. The brakes squealed and smoke billowed up from the rails and the train finally coughed to a stop. A few people laughed like, *That was close.* A guy leaned out the window, looked up and down the tracks, then popped back in, shaking his head. I just sat where I was, aware of the boy again. I didn't want to draw attention to myself.

For two hours the train had been full of strangers, but now everyone was talking to everyone else. A tree down? A mechanical failure? The lady behind me lowered her voice and mentioned a suicide she'd heard about some years earlier. The man in the hat grumbled that he was going to miss an appointment if things didn't get moving.

Eventually, the conductor came through the car and explained there'd been a rockfall, and the tracks were blocked.

It seemed like good news. Maybe I'd get to see Malou and Sara again.

"Will we be turning back to Hope?" I asked. He laughed as if I was making a joke.

"Hardly. It'll take at least an hour to fix this mess. You can get off the train, but stay close. You hear two whistles, a long and a short, that means we're leaving." He walked through the car, saying the exact same thing to everyone he passed.

The train got muggy pretty fast. I was worried about sweating all over Lorraine Welsh's aqua linen suit, and then I remembered it wasn't Lorraine's anymore. It was mine. It was almost new, and so were the matching shoes and the slacks and the short set and the two other dresses Mrs. Welsh had given me after the fire. I didn't want Lorraine to come home from her trip to Europe and be upset because her clothes were gone, but Mrs. Welsh said she'd be delighted to see them put to good use. She'd even insisted I stay in Lorraine's room for a couple of nights rather than in *that awful old church hall* with the other girls. After the *trauma of the fire*, she said, I needed a good sleep.

I looked out the window. I could see a splash of blue through the trees. A lake or a river, not that far off. Mrs. Welsh had really tried. I was starting my adult life now, she'd said. I should look like a lady. She gave me lipstick and mascara and rouge and showed me how to put them on. Then she drove me to the train station in that big green Cadillac of hers and got my luggage out of the trunk. Just as I was about to go, she said, *You know you're always welcome here, dear.*

She leaned in to kiss my cheek, which she'd never done in all the time I'd worked for her, even at Christmas, and I don't know what came over me. I put my arms around her and hugged her, hard. Next thing I knew, I was bawling. When she finally disentangled herself, I immediately knew Mrs. Hazelton was right—I really was just a girl from the Home. Mrs. Welsh's face spelled that out in great big letters for me.

I did my best to pull myself together. I thanked her for the suitcase and the lovely clothes and letting me stay with her, and then I walked away. Tears were streaming down my cheeks like a pot boiling over, but I had no way to turn down the heat.

I'd tilted my face back to stop the flow, and that's when I saw the boy for the first time. He was in the train, looking out the window at me. I turned away and hurried into the station to buy my ticket.

Now, two hours later, the train was practically empty. People were standing in the shade, smoking or hunched on the ground changing babies' diapers or just pacing up and down beside the tracks, fuming about missed meetings. The boy had disappeared.

If I went down to the lake, I could splash a little water on my neck, take off these ridiculous stockings. I left my stuff on my seat and stepped outside. The woods smelled good, like long walks with Sara, cutting down the Christmas tree or the time Joe piled us all in the back of his truck and took us berry picking at Sinclair Ridge.

I wasn't going to let myself think about that.

I wasn't going to think about Joe at all, or the look on his face when we said goodbye. My purse was on the train and my hankies were in it, and if I thought of him at all, I knew I'd start to cry again.

I slid down the embankment toward the water. As soon as I was out of sight, I took off my shoes and stuffed my stockings into them. The moss under my bare feet reminded me of something I thought was good at first but then realized wasn't.

Running out of the Home in my pajamas. The grass mercifully cool after the heat of the fire.

I wasn't going to think about that either.

The trees thinned out toward the lake. As I got closer, there were mostly wild-rose bushes and some other thorny thing I didn't know the name of but knew could ruin my suit if I wasn't careful. I held my skirt up so it wouldn't get snagged, and waded through the bushes.

There was a boulder hunched on the shore. I'd just scrambled up onto it when water splashed my legs, and the boy's head popped out of the lake.

"Hey!" he went. "You spying on me or something?" He swung his bangs off his forehead and launched himself up onto the rock beside me.

I turned and ran.

I could hear him going, "Just kidding! It was a joke!" but that only made it worse. Of course it was a joke. Anyone would know that.

I grabbed my shoes and beat it all the way back to the train. I didn't worry about thorns or brambles or my fancy new clothes anymore. I just kept thinking I'd made a fool of myself and that he did have freckles. A lot. Even more than me. His shoulders were covered with them, and the tips of his ears too.

I leaned back in my seat with my hand on my chest and blood pounding in my face. I could have told Mrs. Hazelton this type of thing would happen if she made me go. All those years she was so worried about my heart, and then she went and did this to me.

"You'll be fine," she'd kept telling me in her study. "You're a smart girl. You can sew. People always need seamstresses."

And then, of course, when none of that had worked, she'd said, "You don't have a choice, Dot. We're not rebuilding the Home—the province is closing down the orphanages anyway. We'll do our best to foster out the Little Ones, but the big girls have to leave. The seven of you have to look after yourselves now."

When I asked again where she expected me to go, she did the same thing as before. She started fussing with the coat.

"*Howell's of Buckminster.*" She was back to reading the label. "*For the discerning gent.* Oh dear…I should have had this cleaned." She scratched at the mildew on what was left of the three letters embroidered on the inside pocket. "These must have been the owner's initials, but the last one's all but gone now. I can read *E* and *B*, then…I don't know. *R? N? A?* Could be almost anything, I guess."

I turned my face into my shoulder and rubbed away the tears. The smoke from the fire had seeped into my skin. I smelled like a weenie roast.

When I looked up, Mrs. Hazelton was staring at me with her head tilted and her eyebrows raised. "This could be the key to your future, don't you think?"

I had no idea what she meant. "What? You want me to go work as a seamstress at"—I checked the label—"Howell's of Buckminster?"

Wrong answer.

She adjusted her posture and tried again. "There are laws regarding adoption, Dot. Parents give up their children with the understanding that their identity will be kept secret. Many have good reasons for never wanting to see the child again."

She took the lid off the teapot to see how much was left, then poured herself a cup.

"Other people aren't so sure. They're just trying to do what's best for the child. People like that often leave behind a…" She circled a hand in front of her, but I didn't know the word she was looking for.

"…a token of some sort. A Bible, maybe, or a locket. A little something to let the child know this was done out of love. Sometimes though"—she poured a thin dribble of milk into her tea—"the token seems an awful lot like a clue. One baby arrived here with a torn ticket to a dance hall pinned to her dress. Another came with a photo tucked into her bunting bag. It was of a man—a boy, really—wearing a hockey jersey, the name of the team on the front, a sign for the arena in the background. The only thing missing was his phone number."

She cleared her throat. "And then, of course, there was this one newborn who arrived wrapped in an expensive coat complete with the store label and the initials of the man who owned it."

Everything went quiet and sort of sparkly. I looked at the coat. I looked at Mrs. Hazelton. Her hand was hovering over the sugar bowl, as if she was trying to decide between one lump or two.

"Are you saying my parents"—the word was so strange—"want me to find them?"

She took two lumps and stirred them in. The tinkling of her spoon seemed way too cheerful for the situation.

"I'm not saying anything of the kind. I heard someone pounding on the door one night. I came downstairs and found a baby. I looked up and saw a dark car speeding off down a dark road. I have no idea who left you, why they left you or what they meant by leaving these things with you. Even if I did, I wouldn't tell you. As I said, I'm not legally allowed to disclose the identity of parents."

Mrs. Hazleton had always been so straightforward. *Stay. Sit. Roll over.* Now she was going around in circles. Perhaps she could tell it was starting to annoy me.

She folded her hands on the edge of the desk, like a kid waiting for roll call. "I will tell you, though, that as a rule, babies are left on the doorstep under cover of darkness because someone's trying to hide something, usually themselves. You, on the other hand, arrived with what amounted to a mailing label."

She flipped open the coat again and started reading. "*Ten Queen Street, Buckminster, Ontario.* All I needed was an envelope and a stamp and I could have sent you back by return post. Make of that what you will."

She paused to make sure I understood.

"And there's another thing I know too. I know you. I know you'd be better off trying to track down the truth than continuing to let your imagination run wild—although you'd never get me to admit that in public."

She finished her tea and settled into her chair, her job done.

Great, I wanted to say, *and just how exactly do you expect me to get myself to Buckminster? How am I supposed to pay for this little investigation?* I'd kept all the money I'd earned at the Welshes in an old jam jar under the bed, and we both knew what had happened to that.

I wanted to scream at her, but I didn't. She pulled her thin beige cardigan around her chest. She looked tired. Betty had told me Mrs. Hazelton was sick, but I hadn't believed it until then.

I shrugged, nodded, did something with my face that looked vaguely like *sure, why not*.

She nodded too, then reached into her top drawer and laid a thick white envelope on the desk in front of me.

⁓

The long and the short whistle sounded. People climbed back onto the train, laughing and chatting.

It could have been the happy noises everyone was making, but I felt calmer. Even the sound of the boy whistling as he got on board was almost okay. (What difference did it make? I'd get off the train and never see him again.)

I thought of Joe. When I'd gone to say my goodbyes, he was packing up his things. He'd worked at the Home since before I was born, and now he had to go too. He'd laughed at my sad face and said, *C'mon, girl. There's only a screen door between* scared *and* excited. *Time you stopped worrying and walked on through.*

He was right. Why shouldn't I be excited?

Mrs. Hazelton had given each of the Seven an envelope with $138 in it to *see us on our way.* I had a brand-new wardrobe. I was on a train to Buckminster.

And there was a tall man missing a cashmere coat and a sterling-silver mustard spoon who just might like to meet me.

Two

TWO HOURS LATER, I found myself on the *scared* side of Joe's screen door again.

I was perched on the crossbar of a blue CCM bicycle as the boy from the train double-rode me up Highway 7 toward Lake McKie.

That was absolutely the last thing I'd expected to happen when I arrived in Buckminster that afternoon. I'd almost forgotten about him. I'd been lost in this crazy idea that all I had to do was go to Howell's, find my father and begin our happy life together.

It didn't work out that way.

Long story short: there is no Howell's in Buckminster—hasn't been since the war.

At least, that's what the man who ran the pet store at 10 Queen Street told me after we cleared up our little misunderstanding over whether I was looking for Howell's or owls.

(He found that way funnier than I did. He kept saying his wife was going to have a real *hoot* over that one.)

It was five o'clock by then. The man said if I wanted menswear, I'd have to try the Dads 'n' Lads Shoppe on Prince Albert Street the next day, and then he locked up the store and left to catch the tail end of his son's canoe regatta. I slumped on his front step and tried to figure out what to do.

My new shoes were killing me. My so-called clue was useless. I wanted Sara.

Across the street was a yellow brick building with a sign that read *Maple Leaf Inn—Klean, Komfortable, Kourteous!* I decided I'd get a hotel room for the night. I'd think better with clean feet and a couple of Band-Aids.

The man at the desk said he had a single room with a lovely view of the Okanoka River. It cost four dollars, which I knew was extravagant but thought was doable—until I opened my purse and realized the envelope with all my money was gone.

I ran all the way back to the train station—my neck straining like a sled dog's, my suitcase banging at my knees—but by the time I got there, the place was closed for the day.

Not that it would have made any difference.

I knew the envelope hadn't fallen out of my purse. I knew it wouldn't end up at the lost and found. Someone had taken it while I was down at the lake. I knew that as surely as I knew what an idiot I'd been for leaving my purse on the seat in the first place.

I could feel tears beginning to sizzle on the underside of my eyeballs. Once again, I hadn't kept my wits about me. Once again, I'd made a mess of things.

I sat on the steps of the deserted train station with my knees together and my feet apart and my head in my hands, and I thought of everything I'd lost. My home. My friends. My money. My job. I had nothing left except some fancy clothes, and I couldn't have cared less about them.

I let the tears splat onto the scuffed brown steps. None of the other Seven had even tried to stay. No one had said, "We don't need the Home. We can work something out together." We'd hugged and cried, but then everyone had just taken off. Everyone had better things to do than stay with me.

I thought about that for a long time. Then I stood up, wiped the tears and snot and last smudge of lipstick from my face, and thought, Fine.

Fine.

Throw me out. Look down on me. Ditch me. Rob me blind. I don't care.

I grabbed my suitcase and started walking back downtown. I'd been ditched before. Dumped on some doorstep in the middle of the night in nothing but some guy's moldy old coat. I'd survived. I could do it again.

I just wasn't sure how.

Something would come to me.

I kept walking.

The shops in Buckminster were closed, and the sidewalks almost empty. I passed a couple of men strolling home with their hats set back on their heads and damp gray patches spreading across their chests. A family in sandals jostled through the door of the Esquire Café, everyone laughing and jockeying for position. A white-haired lady shooed a bunch of girls in flowered shorts off the steps of the Memorial Library. They spilled onto the sidewalk, breaking around me like a school of minnows splitting up to dodge a weed.

There was a little park at the end of the main street with a war cenotaph and benches. I sat down to rest my feet, but my eyes wandered over to a community bulletin board.

A job. I could get a job.

I jumped up and riffled through the notices. Most of them were about missing cats and strawberry suppers and nearly new rowboats available for sale or rent, but then I spotted a yellow sheet almost hidden right at the bottom.

Now hiring, it said. *Waitresses required immediately. Room and board provided. Apply at Dunbrae Arms, just off Highway 7 on Lake McKie. Ask for Mrs. Smees.*

A lady in Gina Lollobrigida sunglasses pointed me toward the highway, and I headed off.

I'd never been a waitress before, but I'd cleared the table at the Home every night since I'd been big enough to carry a plate without tipping over. I figured I could do it.

I took a big breath. This was going to be okay.

Buckminster petered out into gas stations, vegetable stands and the odd chip wagon. There was a T-intersection at the edge of town with a billboard showing a pin-up girl speeding off in her pink bikini and matching motorboat. *Come again to beautiful Buckminster*, she was apparently saying. *Capital of Cottage Country!*

After that, it was just blue sky, yellow fields and the hot, black strip of Highway 7.

I hoped I'd see a sign soon for the Dunbrae Arms, but that was before I did see one and realized I had six miles to go. The sun was getting lower, and my shadow longer and weirder. I thought about how it made my head look like the Bride of Frankenstein's and how there was no way I'd get to Dunbrae Arms before midnight and how there was nothing I could do about it. I dabbed at my blisters with my hankie and kept walking.

Sara and I'd had this thing. We used to stay up late, working on our sewing projects, talking, laughing. We'd pooled our money and bought a transistor. We kept it low so we wouldn't wake the Littles, but every time "Runaway" came on, we couldn't help it. We'd get up and dance.

That's what was in my head now. That song.
As I walk along, I wonder
what went wrong...
My little runaway
a run-run-run-run-runaway.

It was like a cruel joke. Some runaway I was. Throwaway, more like. But it had a beat, and it kept me going, so I plodded along to it.

I was way outside of town before I stopped for a break. It must have been around seven but still hot. I took off my jacket and opened my suitcase to stuff it inside.

And there was the coat.

Joe had wrapped it in an old plastic sheet so the mildew wouldn't spread through my clothes. It was just taking up room, weighing me down. I should throw it out, I thought.

Something about that struck me as monumentally tragic. I crouched on the highway shoulder, staring into the suitcase like I was staring into the casket of my beloved. What good was it to me now? There was no Howell's. My one hope of finding my parents was gone. I didn't even have my letters.

My letters.

I put my hand over my mouth.

I knew I was being ridiculous. But all orphans are, when it comes to stuff like this. We all had something. Some dream, some delusion, some proof—ha!—of our real parents. For me, it was the letters.

It'd started six or seven years earlier. Christmas at the Home was always a bit of a crapshoot. People from town would just go and buy something that more or less looked like a present. They'd slap some wrapping paper on it, mark it with a tag (*Suitable for 10- to 12-year-olds*), then scratch *good deed* off their holiday to-do list.

Occasionally, you'd get something decent, like a bag of humbugs or a bunch of *Archie* comics. Way too often, though, you'd tear open your gift to find a three-pack of cotton underpants, which were always enormous but, as such, at least good for a laugh.

That Christmas, I got a box of pink notepaper and matching envelopes. Printed at the top of each page, in big swoopy letters, was *Thinking of you...*

Toni cracked up. "Thinking of who exactly? We're orphans. Who the hell are we going to write to?"

She had a point. Frankly, I'd rather have gotten the ten-gallon panties. I put the notepaper under my bed and tried to forget about it.

But every night as I was going to sleep, I'd find myself picturing the same thing: Joe walking up from the mailbox, saying, "Well, lookie here. A letter for Miss Dorothy Blythe."

It started out as a little game, a way to fill a boring afternoon when I was sick in bed with bronchitis. I got out the notepaper and wrote myself a letter from Queen Elizabeth, who was youngish and pretty and apparently desperate to find her beloved long-lost daughter—i.e. me. I put the letter in an envelope and slipped it under my mattress.

Every now and then, when no one was around, I'd take it out and read it, as if it had just arrived in the mail. It was so perfect, I'd almost forget I'd written it myself.

I had bronchitis a lot that year. Her Highness never came to rescue me, so I chose someone else. (One benefit of being an orphan: disposable parents.)

Later, I moved beyond moms and dads. I saw Sandra Dee in a movie. When I realized she was too young to be my mother, I made her my sister. Then she introduced me to her co-star, Bobby Darin, who, naturally enough, fell madly in love with me from afar. (His letters got pretty steamy, although on rereading them later, it was clear I had absolutely no idea what the word *screwing* actually meant.)

When I'd gone through all the notepaper, I bought myself a new box.

Pathetic, I know. Some of the other girls were flirting and kissing and what have you with real boys, and here I was, still playing with my imaginary friends. But I couldn't help myself. I'd get lonely or mad or worried about something, and *bingo*, what would arrive but an adoring letter from my dad or my mother or some famous teenage heartthrob who only had eyes for me.

I wasn't nuts. I knew the letters weren't real. But still. Watching the fire rip through our room that night and knowing all those people from my past were disappearing with it kind of killed me. That whole part of my life was gone. I couldn't throw out the coat too.

I was trying to snap the suitcase shut and thinking about stuff like that and not fully keeping my wits about me when I realized a cool black shadow had fallen over me.

"I thought that was you," the boy from the train said, and I leaped over the suitcase as if I'd been hurled from an ejector seat.

"Whoa!" he went. "What are you, a toad or something?" He was sitting high on his bike, eyebrows gone all funny, lips rippling back and forth between laughter and horror. "Seriously. You're like a toad."

"Gee. Thanks," I said. I scrambled up and pushed my hair off my face and squished my foot back into Lorraine's shoe and did my best not to look at him any more than I absolutely had to. His shirt was unbuttoned. He was taller than I'd thought.

He waved his hands at me, palms out. "No. No. Just in terms of jumping, I mean. As far as I can tell, that's your only toad-like quality." He took another look at me. "Except maybe the way you're holding your mouth right now."

I immediately did something different with my mouth, which made him laugh even harder. He hunched over his handlebars, big hands dangling off the ends, head bouncing.

I think he was saying, "That's worse," but it was difficult to tell, what with the gasping and everything. I picked up my suitcase and dragged my bleeding dignity away from the scene of the crime.

After a while I couldn't hear him except in my head, which was almost as bad, but then there was that sweeping sound tires make on pavement and his shadow crept up on me again.

"Sorry," he said. "Sorry." His voice sounded really serious and halfway down his throat, the way people's voices do when they're worried they're going to crack up if they're not careful.

I kept walking.

"I mean it." He reached out and put his hand on my bare arm, and this time I didn't do anything toady.

I did that thing frogs do when you shine a flashlight into their eyes—they go into a death trance (and usually pee, which, mercifully, I didn't do).

"Look. You see a pretty girl crouched on the side of the road, you don't expect her to suddenly, like, catapult herself through space. I was just surprised"—he shrugged, looked cute—"and in my surprise, I mistakenly said *toad*. Which I realize now was a poor choice of words."

More shrugs, more cute.

I tried to get going again, but he'd steered his bike in front of me and was blocking my path. Boys' belly buttons have hair in them. I'd never realized that before.

"Not just because it could be misconstrued as insulting, if you didn't know how much I in fact *like* toads—but also because it doesn't do you justice."

The sun was hitting his face in a way that turned one eye as green and see-through as a 7-Up bottle. The whiskers on his cheek looked like grains of sand. He had a small chip in one of his otherwise perfect front teeth. I made myself focus on the chocolate bar in his shirt pocket instead.

"Because, whoa. That was some jump. No mere reptile could have done that."

"Toads are amphibians."

"Right." He laughed. "Good point."

For years, *Know Your Swampland Creatures* was my favorite library book, which, of course, is absolutely no excuse for ever quoting it, let alone at a time like this.

"No mere *amphibian*. Exactly. I should have said you're like"—he scanned the sky for a better example—"like Catwoman or Wonder Woman or something."

He thought I was an idiot. You'd only say something like that to a person you knew for a fact was a moron.

"Excuse me," I said, "I have to be going," and I tried to step around him.

"Ach. Be going where?" he said, in some sort of leprechaun accent. Why was everything I did funny? He looked down the empty highway. "Where could you possibly...*be going?*" That accent again.

I considered lying, but I'm not very good at it, least of all when a boy is looking at me with his eyelashes still wet and stuck together from laughing at the last thing I've done.

"The Dunbrae Arms," I said and did get past him this time. He turned his bike around and started coming after me, one foot pushing along the pavement like a barge pole.

"You're walking there?" I was apparently weak in the head. "In kitten heels?"

That almost made me laugh—a boy with messy hair and wrinkled chinos actually knowing what kitten heels were— so maybe I smiled a bit.

Somehow he was in front of me again and doing that winking thing he'd done on the train. I curled my shoulders forward and sort of muffled a laugh into my neck, which Toni was always telling me not to do because it made me look mentally deficient and it's bad enough being from the Home without appearing like there was some reason you were put there in the first place.

He stuck out his hand and said, "Eddie Nicholson." I stared at it for a second, then put down my suitcase, and we shook. "Dot Blythe," I said.

He said, "What?" so I said, "Dot. Like Dorothy," and that was apparently funny too.

He said, "Oh. Okay, *Dot*...give me your suitcase."

I said, "Why?"

He pulled back his chin like it was so obvious and said, "I'm double-riding you there."

I didn't answer—only because I couldn't, not because I agreed—but he smiled like, *All right then.* He got me to hold the bike while he figured out how to strap my suitcase onto the back. When he'd rigged something up with his belt and a bit of twine he had in his pocket, he got on his seat, put his hands around my waist and went, "Okay. Up you go."

He had his arms on either side of me, and every breath he took sent goose bumps up my neck, so pretty soon it felt like all the skin on my whole body was pleated behind my ears. I'd never been on a bike before. I'd never been that close to a boy before (regardless of what Bobby Darin implied in his letters). I'd never felt so far away from the Home before.

Someone honked as they drove by. Eddie waved and the bike swerved and I fell back, and the whiskers on his chin grazed my shoulder and made me think of sand again. Then he swerved to avoid a pothole, and we bumped into each other and he went, "Whoa!" Then he swerved another time, even though the road was perfectly flat and no one was driving by. That's when I figured out he was doing it on purpose.

I went, "Hey," and he said, "Took you long enough."

A little later he said, "You smell good," and I thought I was going to die until he added, "All smoky. Like bacon or something." I was afraid he was going to realize I was one of the girls who'd escaped the fire at the Home and drop me on the side of the road right then and there, but he just asked if I wanted to split his Malted Milk. He tore open the wrapper with his teeth and snapped the bar in two without even waiting for an answer. Then he asked me, mouth still full, if I was going to work at the Arms, and I nodded. He asked me if I'd missed my ride or something, and I nodded again. (The *or something* part meant I wasn't lying.) He wondered if my parents would be worried. (I shrugged, which was vague enough not to be lying either.)

And that's the way it went. He talked. I nodded, shook my head or shrugged. It was hard to keep my wits about me. Eddie smelled like fresh laundry and chocolate and Ban deodorant and way better than I was led to believe boys would smell.

I don't believe I'd ever encountered anything that terrifying in my entire life, and I'm including the fire when I say that.

Three

I MUST HAVE said thanks. No way I'd have let him double-ride me for a good five miles and not said thanks.

Would I?

I don't remember. Eddie took me right to the front door of the lodge—that's what he called it—tipped the bike over and sort of pitched me off. Just before I tumbled onto the gravel, he caught me around the waist. My hand gripped his arm—warm and solid—and I felt like I'd discovered a whole new species.

"Whoops. Almost lost you," he said.

I stood myself up and patted down my skirt and moved my mouth around my face without managing to do much else with it.

He twisted back, like the discus thrower from that book on Ancient Greece I'd taken out six times before the librarian suggested someone else might like to read it, and undid my suitcase. "Must be meeting Mrs. Smees, are you? You know where?"

I don't know what my face did then, but he said, "She's not that bad. Go downstairs to the basement and it's two, maybe three, doors to the right."

He passed me my suitcase. I held it in front of me and stared at the little gold stripe on the handle.

He said, "So how about I take you for a ride around the lake sometime?"

I no doubt emitted some sort of squeak at that and was maybe preparing to say thank you then, but by the time I could make myself look at him, Eddie was riding up the driveway, his shirt ballooning out at the sides, his bike ticking back and forth between his legs like a windshield wiper in a downpour.

I asked myself if I was making him up. It's the type of thing I'd do and, frankly, the only logical explanation for him. I turned away before he disappeared into a puff of smoke.

The lodge was a fancy, four-story stone building with a wide driveway, flowers everywhere and a big engraved sign out front saying *Welcome to the Dunbrae Arms* that somehow made me feel exactly the opposite.

A man with gold piping on his shoulders opened the door for me and smiled. He was somewhat less nice when I said I was there for the waitressing position. He jerked his head toward a staircase and said, "One floor down. Housekeeping," then turned his smile on again for a man coming through the door with a red face and a tennis racket.

I crossed a big hall with a high ceiling and a chandelier made out of antlers. The floors gleamed. I imagined this was the type of place the Welshes went to on holidays.

A door straight ahead swung open, and a red-haired girl in a green uniform came flying out. She had an ear pressed hard against her right shoulder to make room on her left for a big black tray loaded with greasy stacks of thick white plates. A fork fell off and clanged against the floor, but the girl kept going.

A couple of seconds later, a blond girl bolted out, carrying an armload of tablecloths. She was sucking on her lower lip, laughing about something she clearly shouldn't be. She saw me looking, wiped whatever was amusing her off her face and chased after the first girl.

The stairway to the basement was tucked away on the right. I carried my suitcase the first few steps, then thumped it down the rest of the way. Everything was perfect upstairs, but down here it was just bare floors, bare lightbulbs and the smell of laundry detergent.

Eddie was right. A sign on the third door said HOUSEKEEPING, and underneath, in flaky black paint, M. Smees. I knocked once.

"Yesssss." The woman sounded as if she'd already had enough of me.

I stepped into a big room cluttered with piles of papers, folded sheets and, along the back wall, canvas bags shored up as if someone was bracing for a flood. In the corner, half hidden by a massive heap of laundry, was an old Singer sewing machine just like the ones we'd had at the Home.

In the middle of the room was a skinny woman, sitting at a desk, typing.

"Mrs. Smees?"

"What is it?" She didn't look up.

"I'm here about the waitressing position."

She stopped typing. She flipped up the watch safety-pinned to her dress and checked the time.

"At eight in the evening."

"There was a rockfall. My train was late…"

She snorted as if she'd heard that one before and started typing again.

"I got here as soon as I could."

"Not soon enough." Now she looked at me, her mouth turned up into a mean little U. "The positions have been filled."

"But the sign. In town. On the bulletin…"

She slapped her hands on either side of the typewriter, slung her lower lip over her right shoulder and shouted, "Bas!"

There was a half-open door behind her. Someone inside went, "Yup."

"You take down the signs in town?"

"Eldridge was doing that."

She glared at me as if I was in cahoots with this Eldridge guy. Her face had no color and neither did her dress, except under the arms, where there were two chocolate-milk-brown crescents. She shook her head and got back to her typing.

Normally, I'd have been afraid of her but I needed a job. I needed a job *here* because Eddie Nicholson was going to take me on a ride around the lake.

"I'm a good worker," I said.

"Pity you didn't come earlier then. Apply next year."

"I don't have to be a waitress. I could do something else. Anything else. Don't you have anything else?"

"Not for a girl." She licked the end of her pencil and started erasing something she'd written. The light from the desk lamp lit up her hair. It was dull brown and teased thin as a spiderweb.

"Thank you," she said, meaning *beat it, kid.*

I didn't move. I could not leave without a job.

There was a knock, and at exactly the same time the door opened, slamming my suitcase into my shin.

It was the laughing waitress from upstairs, still carrying the armful of tablecloths. She saw me rubbing my leg and mouthed, "Oops," then said, "Mrs. Smees?"

The girl's voice sounded happy, but Mrs. Smees looked up from her typewriter with her eyebrows arched, wicked-stepmother style.

"What now, Rathburn?"

"Mr. Oliphant sent me down here. I have"—she bit her finger—"a small problem." She lowered the tablecloths. Her uniform was ripped wide open at the seam from armpit to waist.

"What in the name of hell-o did you…?" Mrs. Smees was up and wiggling her skinny hips past the piles of linen.

"Goofing around, no doubt. You don't get a tear like that folding napkins or restocking the cutlery trays, that's for damn sure."

She grabbed the girl's arm and pulled it up as if she'd just declared her welterweight champ. Mrs. Smees studied the rip for a second, then threw the waitress's arm back down.

"Small wonder the seam blew. Even them floozies hanging outside the Legion Saturday night would be ashamed to wear something this tight."

The girl tucked her lips into her mouth, but the laugh escaped through her nose.

"Funny, is it?" Mrs. Smees flicked her chin at her. "Funny? I've got 126 members of the Knights of Arundel upstairs for their annual dinner. I've got 126 orders of Baked Alaska to be brought steaming to their tables in"—she checked her watch again—"four minutes and here you are, uniform torn to bejeezus, one *bosom* busting out for all the world to see—"

The girl made her mouth into a little circle as if she was shocked by the language.

Mrs. Smees's eyes went as slitty as buttonholes. "Always the smart one, aren't you? So what do you suggest I do? Send you back in looking like a stripper and give them poor old men heart attacks? Make the other girls do your section too and just pray they get them Baked Alaskas served before they're all melted into soup? Huh?"

The girl rubbed her chin. "Gee. Maybe if you hadn't spent so long telling me off, we'd have had time to tape the hole shut or something, but now…" She flipped over her palm and gave a pained smile.

A vein on Mrs. Smees's neck pulsed, as thick and pink as an earthworm. "So help me, Glennie Rathburn. I don't give a good goldarn who your Right Honorable father is. This is the—"

"I can fix it," I said.

The girl blinked like, *Really?* Mrs. Smees turned and scowled at me.

"I can do that up in a second." I was already moving toward the sewing machine. "Just take it off."

The girl peeled out of her dress and tossed it to me. She didn't seem the least bit embarrassed to be standing there in the middle of the room, all va-va-voom flesh and pink underwear. Mrs. Smees squawked and threw a tablecloth over her.

The rip was big but not hard to fix. I lined up the edges and sewed it together in a jiffy. I tossed the uniform back to the girl, who dropped the tablecloth—Mrs. Smees squawked again—and stepped into it.

"Seams are pretty frayed," I said. "If I had a little more time, I could patch it, maybe, and…"

Mrs. Smees wasn't listening. She was holding up Glennie's arm, checking my handiwork. She reached into the front of her dress, pulled a little pair of scissors out of her brassiere and snipped off a thread. She gave Glennie a little push. "Now get going. But report back here the second your shift is done. And I mean it."

Glennie craned her head around Mrs. Smees and waved at me, a big smile on her face. She was still buttoning her uniform as she headed out the door.

Mrs. Smees stuffed her scissors back down into her bra and went to her desk.

"The hem is coming undone in the back," I said. "I could fix that too."

Mrs. Smees sat down, took off her glasses and rubbed her face. There was a mark the shape and color of a kidney bean on either side of her nose.

"You can sew?" she said into her hands.

"Sew, iron, clean, cook." (The cooking part was an outright lie.)

She leaned back in her chair, took the remains of a cigarette out of the cuff of her sleeve and rolled it between her fingers.

"Who's your father?" She struck a match on the underside of her desk, lit the butt and took a drag. "Anyone I should know?"

"I'm not from here," I said.

"No, none of you college girls are. You're all too good for the likes of Buckminster, aren't you? Doesn't mean your daddies aren't going to be sticking their noses into my business."

"My father won't. I've never known him to do anything like that."

She laughed, flicked a little tobacco off her tongue, stared at me. For some reason—Lorraine's clothes?—I was a lying college girl, no better than Glennie Rathburn. I didn't know if the truth would be worse than that or not.

"What's your name?"

"Dorothy Blythe. They call me Dot."

"Well, Dot"—she spat out the *t* at the end—"you're in luck. Mrs. Casey's been doing our sewing for donkey's years, but her sciatica's acting up, so she's not coming back this summer."

My face bent into a smile, but I unbent it when I realized this wasn't a smiling matter.

"I'll give you one week to prove I didn't make a big mistake hiring you. If I did, you're out on your behind, no questions asked. Until then, it's seventy-five cents an hour, eight to four, Monday through Friday, and any other damn time I need you. Understood?"

I was nodding like the plastic hula dancer on the dash of Joe's truck.

"There's a pile of napkins need mending in the corner. Work on those until Rathburn shows you where you're sleeping. Tomorrow I'll get you going on bedspreads and her uniform—if I don't come to my senses and fire her before then."

She licked her fingers and put out her cigarette.

"Now get to work," she said, but it didn't come out as nasty as it sounds.

Four

IT MUST HAVE been ten thirty or eleven before Glennie Rathburn made it back down to the housekeeping office. Mrs. Smees told her to take me to the seamstress's cabin.

"Do your best not to corrupt her in the two and a half minutes it takes to get there, if you don't mind. And here." She pushed a green Dunbrae uniform at me. "You got lucky again. Only one left, and it's an extra small. Didn't want you blaming me for messing up them fine clothes of yours."

Glennie led me out what she called the servants' entrance at the backside of the lodge and up toward the parking lot. The evening had finally cooled off. Everything smelled clean and sort of familiar. There were the sounds of our feet and the buzz of crickets and somewhere across the lake a man laughing, but otherwise the night was quiet.

"Hungry?" Glennie pulled two chicken drumsticks out of her hip pocket and handed me one, still warm and slippery as a newborn puppy. "Most of the food here is crap, but, I must say, their *coq au vin* is downright passable."

I tried to refuse, but she insisted. "Take it. I owe you. I'd have purloined a few more, but Earl was cooking tonight. Poor man's got a brain the size of a bedbug, but boy, eyes like an eagle. I put my life on the line just to get these."

She wolfed hers back in a couple of bites, then wiped the grease off her face with the heel of her hand. You don't expect girls who look like her to act that way.

"So what did you think of Smees? Isn't she a howl? Can you believe how mad she got? It's, like, a ripped seam. Who cares?" She tossed the bone on the ground.

"Oh, geez. Almost forgot. I'm supposed to be giving you the guided tour. Okay"—she pointed like a model in a car commercial—"to our right, the lodge. The beach is in front of the lodge. The parking lot behind."

She beetled ahead of me, then stopped at a walkway cut through a tall hedge running the length of the lawn.

"And here, deep in the bowels of the ninety-fourth circle of hell, is what we lovingly refer to as the Feudal Colony."

We walked through the entrance into a sort of compound. A couple of shabby two-story buildings. A clothesline between them drooping with bathing suits. A truck parked beside a picnic table and a garbage can.

"Hovel A—to your left—is the Meat Department, where out-of-town male employees hang their hats. Don't ever step inside without a chaperone—unless you're damn sure you can get away with it. Hovel B—to your right—is the Harem, but take note: Smees will have a conniption if she hears you call it that. In her imaginary world, we're all proper young ladies with no interest whatsoever in the opposite sex. And this"—she turned toward a small wooden shed half hidden behind a scraggly lilac bush—"is the seamstress's cabin. Sorry. I've no suitably scandalous nickname for it. Mrs. Casey appeared to live quite a virtuous life, at least compared to the rest of us."

She took a key out of her pocket and wiped off the chicken grease before handing it to me.

"I'm such a pig." She smiled, teeth and hair platinum in the dim light, and I could see why she drove Mrs. Smees crazy. Hard not to like Glennie Rathburn.

"Thanks for the food," I said.

"Rob from the rich. Give to the poor..." She bowed humbly, then popped back up. "Oh, my Lord. Love your shoes. Where'd you get them?"

I looked at them, shrugged.

"They're adorable! Linen?"

"I think."

"I die."

"Trade you," I said.

"No! Really? For these old things?"

"Yeah."

I was going to tell her they weren't very comfortable, but she was already toeing off her white sneakers. She slipped a foot into my shoe and pivoted it back and forth like she was about to break into a tap routine. She grinned. "Damn. Now I'm going to owe you again."

She twiddled her fingers goodbye and skipped off, saying something about having to be "shaved, showered and shoveling eggs into the ancient by 7:00 AM."

I climbed up the two steps to the cabin, unlocked the door and fumbled for the light.

Nothing fancy, even by my standards. An old steel bed. An apple crate for a bedside table. An alarm clock. A lamp. And a romance novel held together with an elastic band.

I plunked onto the bed. The springs squeaked and groaned like the old music box Malou and I found behind the woodshed one year. I looked around the room. Last year's calendar was tacked beside the window. August 13 was circled.

Cady's birthday was September 13. I wondered where she was.

I wondered where they all were.

Gone.

I knew that, but I still kept figuring they'd walk in the door any second. I'd shared a room with Sara and Tess for as long as I could remember. We'd all slept, ate, played and had our classes at the Home together. Every day of my life, wherever I was, I could stick out my hand and someone would be there. Sometimes I'd stick it out and they'd slap it away and say, "What now, Dot?" but that was still something.

And now, here I was, alone on the very day I had real news to report. No letters from a pretend boyfriend this time.

I pictured us in our room, lights out. Tess would probably have snuck out the window by then to be with her boyfriend, but Sara would be there. She'd whisper how Luke had showed up at Loretta's for her that day and how much she loved him or how much she hated him, and maybe I'd put in my two cents' worth—I always figured she deserved better than that guy—and then I'd say, "Oh, by the way, I met someone."

Sara would go, "Dot!" and I'd have to shush her before she woke everyone up. I'd tell her how I'd made a fool of myself, taking off like a scared rabbit, and she'd shake her head and say, "I bet it wasn't that bad." And I'd laugh and say, "Maybe—because I ran into him later and he called me pretty and double-rode me all the way to the lodge. And that's not all."

"What?" she'd say. "What? What? What?"

"He's taking me on a ride around the lake." Then we'd squeal into our pillows for a while and spend the rest of the night planning exactly what I was going to wear.

I stared at the cobwebs hanging from the rafters. Looked like the seamstress hadn't cleaned there in years. What *was* I going to wear?

This was going to be okay.

Five

DAYS PASSED WITH no word from Eddie. My bedtime dream conversations with Sara got shorter. Pretty soon I was just staring into the dark, listening to her talk about Luke again. It was okay. I'd always sort of known I wouldn't hear from Eddie.

I'd set my alarm every night for seven, but every morning I'd be awake long before that, blinking at the ceiling, trying to figure out where I was, what I was doing, why. The answers always snuck up on me like bad news, but then the alarm would go off and I'd put on my uniform and just push all that stuff aside.

There was a staff cafeteria attached to the Meat Department, and I'd stop there to grab breakfast. For a while, I was worried about running into Glennie—or worried about *not* running into her, I didn't know which—but none of the waitresses were ever there when I was. Mealtime was their work time. The only people I'd see in the cafeteria were Ida, who ran the place, and the old guys who looked after the grounds. They'd nod at me, faces blank, then go back to their tea and their copies of the *Buckminster Gleaner*.

Mrs. Smees wasn't a whole lot friendlier. She'd give me my orders first thing in the morning, then spend the rest of the day sucking her teeth over whatever she had her dander up about then. She erased the chores blackboard as if it was covered in swearwords. She counted towels as if she'd just caught them trying to escape. She couldn't even be nice nicely. Once, out of the blue, she brought me a sticky bun. Before I could say thank you, she went, "You get one crumb on that linen and so help me…"

The only time she'd soften up was when Bas dropped in from the laundry room next door. He was a little younger than her, maybe thirty-five or so, with a ducktail and matching attitude. He'd lean his bum against her desk and his head against the wall and the two of them would complain about the guests or the bosses or somebody named Dutchie they'd known growing up in Buckminster.

I took Bas for a tough guy. The type you'd see loping home from the foundry with his lunch bucket tucked up under his arm or squirting tobacco juice out the gap between his teeth. The type Mrs. Hazelton always told us to avoid.

I was scared the first time I had to take the mending to him. With the machines all rocking and sloshing, he didn't hear me come in. I couldn't bring myself to call him Bas and didn't know what his last name was, so I just stood there until he turned around. Scared him half to death.

We both screamed. I dropped the mending all over the floor and tried to apologize, but he just put one hand on my shoulder and another on his chest and laughed like I'd got him good.

He helped me pick everything up, then said that if I got behind, he could always come and get it himself, not to worry. He liked the break.

Mrs. Smees hollered to find out where the heck I was, and I started running for the door. Bas went, "Whoa" and pressed his hands down in front of him like he was pushing the air flat. "Slow down, girlie. Let her treat you like that, and she will. Now, walk in there like a lady—and not until you're damn well ready to neither."

So I pretended I was damn well ready and walked in only slightly faster than I would have normally.

At noon most days, Mrs. Smees would say, "What are you waiting for?" then hard on that, "You be back here by 12:45 sharp. No excuses." I'd pick up an egg-salad sandwich from the staff cafeteria, then sit on a log at the far end of the beach and watch.

Even this early in the season, the beach was squirming with kids carrying yellow pails and little blue shovels they were always claiming not to have slapped someone else in the side of the head with. Ladies in bathing suits and earrings sipped pink drinks and played cards at a table near the lodge. College girls lay on their backs, stiff as Barbie dolls, while the hit parade buzzed away on their transistors. Occasionally, they'd flip over to get a better look at the boys in green Dunbrae button-downs tying up boats, filling gas tanks or helping papery old men up onto the dock.

Once I looked over at the lodge and saw Glennie serving guests on the patio. She didn't see me.

I saw Eddie twice.

The first time, I didn't even know it was him. A boat pulled up to the dock and two men in crumpled hats climbed off, carrying fishing poles and wicker baskets. That made me think about Joe and the time he'd taken the Seven trouting, so I didn't notice the guy driving the boat until I heard that laugh, and by the time I realized it was Eddie he was bombing back out into the lake, and all I could see above the spray was his hand shooting out in one last goodbye.

The next time, I was about to head in the servants' entrance when I noticed him giving his arm to an old lady in a bright-red dress and some crazy turban-like thing on her head. She struggled with the patio stairs. "Up you go," he said, just like he'd said to me, and my stomach clenched. I stood there gaping and relieved he hadn't seen the toad face I was no doubt making.

My heart didn't slow down all that afternoon. Until then, I'd never realized that the sound a sewing machine makes is *EddieEddieEddieEddieEddie.*

Since I'd started at the Arms, I'd been working on tablecloths and bedspreads, but around two that afternoon— it was a Friday—Mrs. Smees plunked a canvas bag on the floor and said, "Guest mending. I tagged each garment with instructions."

It was mostly hems and missing buttons, but I figured a bigger project would distract my brain and be better for my heart. I dug around and found a man's tweed jacket with a note on the pocket that said *Torn lining*.

It was the color of porridge and smelled of cigars and some slightly sock-like odor I think of simply as "old man" or, more specifically, Reverend Messervey. I unbuttoned the jacket to check out the tear. The label said *Howell's of Buckminster*.

My breath was sucked down my throat, a Hoover on high.

Mrs. Smees was standing on a stool, changing the list of chores on the blackboard. She spun around and glared at me as if I'd done something wrong. "What?"

"Nothing."

"Don't give me that *nothing* business." She was down on the floor, charging toward me, face like a bayonet. "What?"

"Just, um…"

She snatched the jacket out of my hands, chin bouncing up and down as she scanned it for mistakes. "Yes?"

I'd been caught. I didn't know for what, but I'd been caught. I shrank like a mangy dog who'd just peed on the rug. "Just. It's from Howell's. Like, of Buckminster."

"And that made you gasp?" Eyebrow raised. Suspicious.

"I mean, it must be old, that's all."

"What? Not *that* old. Howell's closed on June 13, 1944, so that's only—" She stopped. Looked out the room's one little window. "Good Lord. That's twenty years."

"You know the exact date it closed?" It just kind of came out.

She huffed. *Of course.* "One week after D-day."

"Oh. That makes it easy to remember, I guess."

"D-day? You think that's easy to remember?" Sometimes, the calmer a person's voice, the scarier it sounds.

"No. Sorry. That's not what I meant."

"You think it's easy to remember all those dead boys?" She kind of laughed, a hot, fast shot of air out her nose. "Boys like Bertie Howell? As if Bertie was the type to storm beaches. Storm anything."

"No. I—"

She leaned in and pointed a finger at me, thin as her lips. "You want to know why I remember? That's why I remember. I was there when Mr. Howell got the telegram saying some Nazi'd splattered his one and only kid all over the coast of Normandy. He closed the store that day. Never came back."

She shoved the jacket at me.

"And look at the work they did." Tapping hard on the lapel with a yellowed nail. "Beautiful. What a waste."

I nodded. I wanted her to stop.

"You know what the sad thing is?"

Sadder than this?

"The war's what made Howell's. Half their business was officer's uniforms. Funny, ain't it? Here Mr. Howell thought Bertie'd be sitting in clover, all the money they was making off the war. Young guys all roostered up at the thought of getting their stripes came from across Ontario wanting their uniforms done up in the finest British wool. A few even got them made out of cashmere, if you can believe it."

"Cashmere," I said, because of course that word meant something to me now.

"Cashmere," she repeated, because of course that was ridiculous. "As if a cashmere greatcoat would make getting your head blown off at nineteen any easier."

She was about to say something else, but her skin bloomed red around her eyes and she stopped midword.

She cleared her throat, straightened her sleeves and turned into Mrs. Smees again. "Whose is that? L.M.B.?" she said, reading the initials on the inside pocket. "Probably Lionel Beals." She sniffed. "It is. Good Lord. Finish it up, then give it to Bas. See if he can get the stink out."

She pushed it toward me, disgusted, no tears in her eyes now.

"Do you know where Mr. Howell is these days?" I said.

"I told you. Gone." She turned her back, hands on hips, and acted like she was reading the blackboard. "What are you so interested in Howell's for anyway? Don't got enough work to do?"

She strutted off.

I shut my mouth, stitched up the lining and thought about my coat. Was it part of someone's uniform?

Did my father go to war?

Was he Bertie Howell maybe?

No. Couldn't be. Bertie died in '44. I wasn't born until '47.

I got out a lady's sundress that needed hemming and tried to think this through. I didn't know much about the war. I'd watched the veterans marching in the Remembrance Day parade every year and seen the ladies dabbing their eyes beside the statue in Hope with the names of all the boys who didn't come back. And, of course, there was Mr. Caswell with the burned face, who worked at Egan's service station. Mrs. Hazelton had torn a strip off us when she caught us staring at the waxy place where his ear used to be. Other than that, all I knew about the war was what I saw in the movies. Mrs. Hazelton had let the Seven go to the Odeon last Christmas and watch *The Great Escape*.

I started imagining my dad as a taller version of Steve McQueen, sitting on his motorbike, smirking, looking the Nazis right in the eye and saying stuff like, *That's a chance you're going to have to take*. That made me happy for a while.

At around three, Mrs. Smees sent me upstairs to see about a torn curtain. The halls along the way were lined with framed photos of the resort and people who'd stayed there. There were pictures of men with twirly mustaches from a 1902 regatta and men in fur coats at a 1924 curling bonspiel and wedding portraits of the Honorable Mr. So-and-So and the lovely former Miss Whatever.

The picture that stopped me, though, was of a 1939 farewell supper for the *officers and gentlemen of Dunbrae Arms*. Thirty or forty men with Brylcreemed hair and big smiles were clowning around in front of the lodge. All of them were wearing coats that looked just like mine.

Impossible to tell if any of them were made of cashmere.

Someone had written the men's names across the photo in white ink. I looked for an E.B. Something, but no hope of that either. They were all nicknames. *Ace Mathers. Pidge Filpots.* Some poor guy called *Sourpuss Kitteridge.*

And who's to say Mr. Something was even in the picture? Thousands of guys from around here had gone to war.

Needle in a haystack, I thought. I got the curtain from the lady cleaning Room 312 and headed back down to work.

❧

Four o'clock rolled around. Mrs. Smees dropped my pay packet on the table and said, "Don't you forget to take that jacket in for cleaning before you go skittering off for the weekend."

When I went into the laundry room, Bas was reading a western, his chin on his chest, his feet crossed on the folding table. "Sorry, Dot. Done my last load for the day. Just throw it in the corner." He nodded over his shoulder without looking up from his book.

I didn't move.

Bas grew up in Buckminster. He was nice. Maybe he'd know.

"Um," I said.

"Yup."

"I..."

He took a stick of Juicy Fruit out of his pocket and stuck it in the book to save his place. "Okay. What?"

"Ah. Know anyone who worked at Howell's?"

"Howell's?"

"Howell's—the men's store."

"I know what it is. Given the tone of your voice, I was just expecting you to ask how to dispose of a body, not *know anyone who worked at Howell's?*"

"Do you?"

"Why d' you want to know?"

"Well...there's this, um...actually I—"

Bas put his hand up like a stop sign. "I've been working in this laundry since I was your age, and I've seen that face plenty of times. You're planning to lie to me. Frankly, I don't really care enough about your business for that. Makes no difference to me what you're up to. I shouldn'ta asked."

I tried not to look too relieved.

"Want to know about Howell's? Muriel Smees's the gal to talk to."

"I did, sort of, but she kind of cut me off."

Bas plunked his feet on the floor, scratched behind an ear with one finger. "Yeah. Come to think of it, that's a scab you might not want to pick. Best not to bring that up again."

"Was Mrs. Smees in love with Bertie Howell?" It suddenly seemed so obvious.

He laughed, one wheezy *ha*. "No. You're way off. She was already with Walter Smees by then. They used to double-date with my oldest sister and that jackass she married. Muriel would have known the Howells pretty good though. She worked at the shop for years. Thinking about what happened to Bertie mighta got her thinking about what happened to Walt, and that's not a happy story neither."

"Was he hurt in the war?"

"Depends what you mean by hurt."

I had a vague idea what he was getting at, enough to know to drop it. "So there's nobody you can think of who worked there?"

"Alive?"

"Yeah." Dead wouldn't help me much.

"Hmm. Tough one. Howell's closed when I was fifteen or something." He puffed out a cheek and thought about it for a second. "Mr. Howell's gone. Grace McFetridge is dead, and Alvin Comeau—he was the tailor there—he's alive, but his mind ain't much anymore. Sits outside the Buckminster Manor for the Aged all day with his mouth hanging open. Poor bugger. Those are the only people I can think of."

I thanked him, threw the jacket on the pile in the corner and headed off for the day.

"I do like me a good mystery though." Bas tucked the stick of Juicy Fruit back into his pocket and reopened his book. "So when you feel like disclosing what you're actually up to, drop by for a chat."

ᕒ

When I arrived at the cafeteria that evening, Ida was just taking meatloaf out of the oven, so I grabbed a plate of that. I needed to be back at my cabin before the waitresses and chambermaids and dock boys got off for the day. That was my routine. Gobble down a meal, go to my cabin, close the curtains and reread that romance novel until I fell asleep.

The other workers would start coming back around seven. Sometimes I'd peek out through the gap between the curtains. It was like watching one of those movies we'd seen in geography class about the traditions of other lands. The kids would be sprawled all over the picnic table or on the scrubby little patch of grass in front of the Meat Department or dancing to music coming from a record player perched in a window. On warm nights, the boys would be shirtless and the girls in bathing suits, even when they were dancing. If things got too loud, someone from the lodge might stomp over to tell them to pipe down, but otherwise the serfs were on their own.

Once, after I'd gone to bed, I heard giggling outside my cabin, and the next thing I knew the door swung open. A couple staggered in. The girl screamed when she saw me, the boy swore, and then they both staggered back out. They apparently thought the seamstress's cabin was empty and knew there was a bed there. After that I locked my door every night.

I finished up the meatloaf and asked Ida if I could take a bowl of tapioca back to my cabin.

"And me lose another dish? You all promise you'll bring your bowls back, then that's the last I ever see of them—unless I find them on the beach or behind the bushes or way back in the woods where none of you people think I know you go."

I nodded an apology and put the tapioca back in the fridge.

Ida took it out again. "You don't seem as bad as the rest." She wiped her hands on the underside of her belly. "But no bowl, no breakfast. Understood?"

We both smiled. I took my dessert and headed down the little path to my cabin. Tapioca wasn't my favorite thing in the world, but it tasted like the Home, and I liked that. If I paced myself, I could make the bowl last right through the final four chapters of *Proudly Rode the Chevalier* by Arabella Castlebury. It seemed like a perfectly good way to spend the night, until I got past the lilac bush and saw a note wedged in my door.

Dot, it read in neat blue writing. *I've been looking for you all week. Ran into Glennie today and she tells me Mrs. Smees has you working in the sweatshop. How about that ride you promised me? I figured since you have certain amphibian characteristics you might like to get out on the water. (I'm anxious to see your frog kick…) What say I meet you on the dock Sunday at noon? I'll make lunch. Eddie.*

Six

I NEEDED SOCKS and I needed something to do until Sunday so I wouldn't explode or float off into the atmosphere like a pink balloon at some little kid's birthday party. I decided to go into Buckminster the next day. The doorman told me the bus came at ten to the hour. I just had to walk up to the highway to catch it.

I opened my suitcase to get some money from my pay packet. Would three dollars be enough for socks and the return trip? I could use new underwear too. The bridal shop in Hope had given us each two sets after the Home burned down, but I was tired of washing them by hand every second night in the staff washroom, and I'd die rather than give them to Bas to do.

So I was thinking about clothes and stores, and maybe that's what got me thinking about Howell's again.

Alvin Comeau was still alive—that's what Bas said—and living in the Buckminster Manor for the Aged. I was going into town anyway. I grabbed the coat and an extra couple of bucks and headed for the highway.

The bus dropped me off by the little park I'd stopped at on the first day. I could see Buckminster Manor from there. It looked like it had been built by the same guy who built the Benevolent Home, or maybe his brother. One little pig built it out of wood. This little pig built it out of stone.

I asked for Mr. Comeau at the desk. I was expecting the lady to grill me about who I was, why I wanted to see him, that type of thing, so I'd spent the bus ride concocting some half-baked story about being a great-niece he'd never met, here from Moose Jaw for a couple of days.

The lady didn't even ask. She just popped up, a grin slung between her ears like a double Dutch skipping rope. "Mr. Comeau? He'll be so pleased!" then, in a whisper, "He's been here since '45, and I swear the old dear hasn't had a visitor in ten years."

She walked me through quiet, dark halls to the back of the manor. The lawn sloped down to the river. Near the bank, a nurse in a crisp white uniform was leaning over a man in a wheelchair parked under a gazebo.

"There he is! Oh, he'll be thrilled." The lady helloooooo-ed to the nurse, who waved me over.

It was a hot day, but Alvin Comeau was in a full dark suit, his head drooping and his tongue hanging out as if he was trying to lick something off his burgundy bow tie.

"Well, Alvie, looks like we have company." The nurse had a good figure, but her lipstick scared me. "What can we do you for?"

"I'd like to have a little chat with Mr. Comeau, if that's okay. About Howell's. Someone told me he used to work there."

"A chat." Her laugh sounded like a car on a cold morning. "A bit late for that. Not much goes in anymore. But have a go at it. He might surprise us."

I knelt down in front of him and tried to catch his attention.

"Mr. Comeau?" His eyes stayed blank, but his lips tried to move. They reminded me of the fatty parts on a boiled ham. "I was given a coat…"

"No, no, no. That's never going to work." The nurse muscled me out of the way and shouted, "ALVIE!" as if she was calling him in from somewhere out behind the barn. "THERE'S MY BOY! YOU GOT A VISITOR. WANTS TO TALK TO YOU ABOUT HOWELL'S."

He lifted his head at that, and she swung her hand toward him like a waiter showing me to a table. "Breathe from your diaphragm and aim at the back of the room. He's deaf as a post."

I knelt back down in front of him and hollered hello. A light turned on behind his pale blue eyes.

"I know you," he mumbled, a long, sticky pause between each word.

"I don't think so," I shouted. "I'm new to town."

"Yes, I do."

"Just smile and nod," the nurse said. "He gets a bit confused."

"I was given this coat." I opened the package and laid it on his lap.

He put his hand on it, looked up at me and smiled. "I made it."

"Yes, you were quite a tailor in your day, weren't you, Alvie? Tell her about the suit you made for the governor general."

Alvie smiled and jawed the air. I didn't want him to tell me about the suit he made for the governor general.

"Did you make many like this?" I yelled.

"Lots. But this is cashmere." That took him about three minutes. "Not many out of cashmere."

"Do you remember who you made it for?"

"The button's broken."

"Yes." I opened it up. "And the lining's torn."

He looked at me and shook his head at this terrible tragedy.

"But it's still beautiful. I found it, and I'd like to return it to its rightful owner." I showed him the initials. "E.B. Something. The last letter's gone. Any idea who that could be?"

He looked for a second like he might know, then shook his head. I took the spoon out of the pocket.

"This was in the coat too. There's a crest on it, says *loyal on the earth*. Or something like that." I showed it to him. "That mean anything to you?"

He raised his finger. "That fellow." He looked at me. He looked at the nurse. Eyes squinting, trying to come up with the name.

"WHICH FELLOW, ALVIE?"

"You know. Good-looking one."

"GONNA HAFTA DO BETTER THAN THAT, SWEETHEART. LOTS OF GOOD-LOOKING ONES, AS I RECALL."

"Big one." He was almost pleading now. "Liked the ladies. Got a medal."

He repeated that a few times, his face edging toward mauve, a little bubble of spit frothing white at the corner of his mouth. The nurse hopped up, stroked his head, calmed him down.

"OH, THAT FELLA. WE KNOW THE ONE. THANKS, ALVIE. YOU WERE A BIG HELP."

End of interview. I could see that.

"Yes, a big help," I said. I reached down to thank him. His hand was dry and spotty. A small hungry animal. It wrapped around mine and pulled me close.

"Nice to see you again." He smiled. "Been a long time."

The nurse rolled her eyes and shouted, "NAPTIME! I'LL JUST SHOW YOUR FRIEND OUT, ALVIE, AND THEN I'LL TAKE YOU TO YOUR ROOM."

"You got more out of him than I ever do," she said walking back to the manor. "I know it wasn't much, but, well, he's not long for this world. I got a couple of ideas about that spoon for you though. Try St. Ninian's Anglican Church.

All the rich people around here get hatched, matched and dispatched there. One of the ladies on the auxiliary is bound to recognize the crest."

"Do you know anyone on the auxiliary I could talk to?"

"Best idea would just be to pop by for one of their meetings. I'm pretty sure they're still Fridays at seven in the church."

"Thanks. And you said you had another idea about the spoon?"

"Melt it down. You could get yourself a nice set of earrings out of it."

Seven

"WELL, LOOK AT you," he said, and call me crazy, but I kind of thought everyone must have been doing exactly that.

It was Sunday at noon. I was on the dock in Lorraine Welsh's turquoise short set and Glennie Rathburn's white runners, and Eddie was on the deck, his hand held up to help me down into a long shiny boat with a little flag snapping at the back. Who on the beach wouldn't be craning their neck to get a look at that? Right out of a movie.

"You bought that shirt because it matches your eyes," he said, and I said, "No."

"Did so."

"Did not."

"Only liars smile like that." And I laughed because I was nervous and because, of course, that was the one thing I wasn't lying to him about.

Eddie untied the boat and we put-putted to the end of the dock.

"Okay. Where to, lady?"

The sky was blue and cloudless, and the water shimmied and sparkled like a majorette's uniform.

"I'd kind of like to see the whole lake."

"The whole lake."

"Yeah."

"Well, we're going to have to hurry then, aren't we?" He grinned, slammed the throttle forward and the boat reared up like the Lone Ranger's horse.

I put my hand on my head to keep my hair from flying clean off my scalp, and I laughed. Water sprayed over the side of the boat when Eddie made a fast turn and splashed over the front when we slapped through another boat's wake. It was cool and the day was hot and nothing could have been more perfect.

Eddie knelt on the driver's seat, head high over the little windshield, shirt puffed up like a football jersey. He'd point and scream at me over the engine. "That's the Burnleys' place. They're loaded." Or "Dead Man. That rock. Sticking out over there. That's what they call it." Or "Go Home Island. Covered in poison ivy."

We passed big mansions surrounded by bright-green lawns, and shabby cabins on islands no bigger than boulders, and shirtless old men in canoes, and kids tipping sailboats, and ladies sunning on inflatable rafts, one leg bent at the knee, and everywhere we went, people waved and went, "Hey, Ed!" or "Nice boat!" or "We seeing you Tuesday?"

Farther on there was a yacht club with a floating dock out front and a bunch of kids jumping off it. Eddie sped in close, then swerved away. The kids hurled themselves into the waves, laughing, screaming, bobbing like empty soda bottles. They were all going, "Eddie! Come back! Do it again!" But he raced off, a crazy smile on his face.

I turned around and looked. The kids were swinging their arms over their heads like we'd marooned them on an ice floe. I could see a splatter of gray roofs in the distance. "Is that Dunbrae way back there?" I shouted, trying to get my bearings.

Eddie leaned down. "What was that?" His face was so close I could smell spearmint and soap and pick out each brown and red and yellow straw of his eyebrows.

I managed to say, "Dunbrae. Is it far?" He nodded, like *really far* and swung back up to the dashboard.

"You don't want to go home already, do you?"

"No," I said, which was true.

"Good." The boat slowed down, flattened out. "'Cause we're almost at Hidden Bay, and it's lunchtime."

We puttered through a narrow passageway, the water so shallow I could see tiny fish darting near the weedy bottom. Eddie's head swayed back and forth as he maneuvered between the rocks on either side. "Got to know what you're doing to make your way in here. That's why nobody ever does."

A boy I didn't know. A place no one went. Mrs. Hazelton wouldn't approve. And I didn't care.

The channel bowed out into a little bay. Everything was still. Willows hanging over the banks. A patch of yellow water lilies. It was like one of those enchanted places children in English storybooks always ended up getting lost in.

Eddie threw the anchor over the side.

"Sit here." He patted one of the seats facing backward.

I sat—and kicked my legs out like a cancan dancer when my thighs hit the hot white leather. We both laughed, Eddie as if he knew that was going to happen.

He opened a picnic basket and pulled out a couple of wax-paper bundles. "Ham or...ham?"

"Well, ham, I guess."

"Wow. Me too. I knew we had a lot in common first time you saw me and ran screaming in the other direction."

"Ha. Ha."

He held up a tartan thermos. "Lemonade or...?"

"I'll have the lemonade, if you don't mind."

"Same here! Why, this is positively eerie."

He handed me a red cup, then slid down into the chair next to me, the scalding seat not seeming to bother him at all.

"Don't suppose we're twins separated at birth or something, do you? One of us adopted into the lap of luxury, the other into a life of grinding poverty."

It was only a joke and it didn't mean anything, but there was just something about it. *Adopted. Orphan. The Home.* I don't know. I choked on my sandwich.

"Y'okay? Do I need to dust off my lifesaving skills?"

I shook my head, took a gulp of lemonade. Mrs. Hazelton was always telling me not to let my imagination run wild. "Good sandwich," I said.

"I can assume, then, that the fact you gagged on it was purely coincidental?" He snickered, stretched his big feet out on top of the cooler and turned his face up to the sun. "So how're you and Mrs. Smees getting on?"

"Oh, you know."

"I told you she wasn't that bad." He took an enormous bite out of his sandwich and stuffed it in one cheek. "I can't believe you fell for it."

I gawked at him. "Could've warned me."

"Then you wouldn't have applied for the job, and we wouldn't be sitting here now. You ask me, a little suffering was worth it."

"'Specially since I'm the one doing the suffering."

He smiled. *I made him smile.* I looked away. I don't know why, but that little chip in his tooth got me every time.

"You know her very well?" I was just filling the air.

"Muriel? All my life. She used to come to the house when I was little. Which is no doubt the origin of my chronic nightmares." He opened his mouth in a silent scream and tore at his hair. He was a goof. I liked that.

"So you grew up here."

"A townie through and through. And my father before me and his father before him. Etcetera. Etcetera."

"Seems like a nice place to live."

He lowered his sandwich and stopped chewing. "You pulling my leg?"

"No. The lake, the town. It's pretty."

He spun his hand like *go on*. "Pretty what? Dull? Deadly?"

"No. Not yet anyway. Just pretty."

"Well, that's a first. You high-class girls always hate it here. I understand there isn't a decent place for miles to get one's hair done." He patted the side of his head, his pinky crooked.

"Not my sort of thing."

"Another first! You're an unusual girl, Dot. A near encyclopedic knowledge of amphibians, a disdain for shallow standards of beauty, a—"

Then suddenly he was standing up and swearing.

"What?"

"You hear that?"

I shook my head.

He swore again, biffed his sandwich into the water, grabbed the anchor.

"What is it?" I thought he was joking.

"Looks like we're in for it," he said, jerking his head over his shoulder. I peered out beyond the bay. The sun was still lighting up the water, but the sky to the right had gone black-eyed purple.

I knew what skies like that meant. Thunderstorm. The Seven all racing to close windows, latch gates, scoop up

Little Ones, get everyone inside before it hit. One year, on a scorcher just like this, we'd lost the barn.

"C'mon, c'mon," Eddie said, either to me or the motor, which didn't seem to want to turn over no matter how much he cursed it.

I pushed the picnic basket into a nook at the back and slid into the front seat. By the time the engine caught, fat blobs of rain were bouncing off the deck and the surface of the bay.

He edged the boat around, and we crawled through the channel. We were the only ones I could see on the lake, but given the way the rain was suddenly coming down in sheets, that wasn't saying much.

He gunned the motor, veered left. "We're not making it back to the Arms in this."

Lightning flashed, and then, seconds later, the thunder, loud and angry. Eddie went, "Yikes," but he was laughing. "That was a little too close for comfort. You all right?"

Maybe for a second there, I looked as if I wasn't. That boom. Like the crack of the rafters when the fire brought down the ceiling. I suddenly remembered everyone screaming, and the smoke and the panic, but that's all it was. A memory. I was okay. I shrugged like it was no big deal. Eddie went, "My kind of girl."

He flicked the water out of his eyes and leaned over the windshield to see. When we came to a big green buoy clanging wildly in the storm, he slowed down, made a hard turn, then headed through a narrow channel. He glided up to a dock, cut the motor and jumped off, the boat still moving.

He was tying it up when lightning, then thunder, hit again. One, two. Fast as that. Right overhead.

"Go, go, go." He dragged me up slick, spongy steps to a cottage, its screen door thrashing against the shingles. He pulled it closed behind us. We skidded through the water on the floor, racing to shut windows, tie back shutters, upturn fallen furniture. Glass pinged in the wind and dishes still rattled, but with the windows shut tight, the sound of the storm wasn't much more than a dull roar. A train in the distance.

And then we were sopping wet and suddenly aware of it, our hair stuck to our faces like spaghetti after a food fight, our arms out to our sides like gunslingers before a duel.

"Sorry," he said.

"What? Why?"

"I should have seen it coming. Not my first time on the lake." The grin. "But you distracted me."

"Sure. Me or the ham sandwich."

"I've had my share of ham sandwiches before. Don't think it was that." I had a sudden urge to inspect my shoes. "Anyway. Welcome to my humble abode."

I looked around—or, at least, away from him. "Nice. Cozy."

But not what I expected. The cottage was old, dark, dusty as a chicken coop. Nothing much to it. A horsehair chesterfield sagging like a fat lady at a bus stop on a hot day.

A table and a couple of mismatched chairs. A big stone fire-place, singed black to the mantelpiece.

Eddie picked a towel off the back of the chesterfield and sniffed it. "Not sure how clean this is." He tossed it to me.

"That's okay." I wiped my face and hair. When I looked up, he was gone.

"Eddie?" I'd never said his name out loud.

"There in a sec."

I was starting to shiver. I'd been so hot, but the rain had gotten right through to my bones.

There was a copy of the *Buckminster Gleaner* on the coffee table, kindling and logs in a barrel by the fireplace. I scrunched up the paper, made a little teepee of wood and was running my hand along the mantelpiece, searching for matches, when Eddie walked back in.

"Well, aren't you a busy bee."

I turned around. His hair was combed like a kid about to have his class picture taken, and he was in dry clothes.

"These are the only things I could find that might fit you." He held up a pair of beige shorts and a matching shirt with badges above the pocket. "I'm sure you'll make a more fetching Boy Scout than I ever did."

He saluted. I laughed. "Where can I change?" He pointed over his left shoulder.

The bedroom was tiny, mostly bed. A twig bookshelf was nailed to the wall, a skinny bureau tucked in the corner. I closed the door, took off my wet clothes and put on the dry ones. The shorts hung off my hips. I hadn't been eating enough. I was a bag of bones. I tucked the shirt in and hoped that would help the shorts stay up.

There was a mirror above the bureau, chipped around the edges and peeling on the back. My reflection was dark and flecked, an old-fashioned photo. Miss Dorothy Blythe circa 1864. By the looks of it, that was around the last time I got my hair done too.

I noticed a picture tucked into the frame. A little boy, laughing, nose crinkled up—clearly Eddie—leaning against a man sitting on a dock. They were both in bathing suits. The man was missing a leg from the knee down. (I looked twice to be sure.) He had a big smile on his face too. I recognized the dimples.

When I went back into the living room, Eddie was rummaging in the fireplace, undoing everything I'd set up. The newspaper I'd used was smoothed out and lying flat on the coffee table. He lit the kindling and blew on it until the flame caught.

"Does this mean I don't get my campfire badge?" I said.

"'Fraid not." He turned around and whistled. "You could teach me to tie knots any day."

I blushed. He apologized. One of us had to stop doing that.

"Make yourself at home. I'll put some cocoa on." He went into the kitchen, turned on the radio and rattled around in cupboards.

I sat on the couch and flipped through the newspaper Eddie'd uncrumpled.

BUCKMINSTER MAN WINS NATIONAL WHITTLING COMPETITION

KINSMEN RAISE $328 TOWARD NEW BANDSTAND

ST. NINIAN'S FASHION SHOW DRAWS CROWDS

I'd almost finished reading before I noticed the articles were by Edward Nicholson.

"You're a reporter?" I said.

"Sort of," he called out from the kitchen.

"I'm impressed."

"Oh, right. You say that, but only minutes ago you were ready to torch my entire *oeuvre*."

"Sorry. I thought it was garbage."

"Close enough."

He'd filled the mugs too full. Cocoa sloshed over the sides. He set them on the coffee table, then licked his hand and wrist. "I just fill in during the summer so the genuine reporters can take holidays. Not my real job."

"You have a real job?"

"'Course."

"Doing what?"

"Following the proud Nicholson family tradition. I'm a caretaker. Look after people's cottages, mow their lawns, take their old aunties to lunch at the Arms when they can't be bothered doing it themselves. I even fill up their fancy boats and take attractive girls out for a spin, just to make sure everything's in working order."

He sat at the other end of the couch and crossed his ankles on the table. His feet were bare, and he was losing a toenail. "Disappointed?" he said.

"Why would I be?"

"Girl like you."

"What are you talking about?"

"I saw you at the train station. Big green Caddy. Tearful goodbye with your elegant mother. Not the type of girl to date a caretaker."

This was a date.

I shook my head. "You're imagining things."

"Hey. Nothing to be ashamed of." He nudged me with his toe, and I could have told him the truth right then and there, but suddenly I liked being Mrs. Welsh's daughter. I liked the way it made him look at me.

"I'm not," I said.

"Take me for a drive in the Caddy someday?"

"If I get a chance."

He'd brought his mug up to his mouth but was smiling too hard to take a sip.

"So are your parents here?" I wanted to know about the man with the missing leg. I had a feeling it would be the type of story I'd like.

"They split up when I was six. Mum lives in Toronto now. I've got a half sister I see as much as I can. Stacy. Ten.

Really cute. That's where I was coming from when I saw you at the station."

"And your dad? He's here?"

"When he's sober."

"Oh."

"Uh-oh. Pity alert!" He made a sound like an air-raid siren.

"Stop," I said, my hands over my ears.

"Okay, then you stop with the sad eyes. I don't get to drive a Caddy—or wear kitten heels—but I got nothing to complain about. Dad had a bad war. He's not a bad guy." He shrugged, took a gulp. "You'd like him. Everyone does. Even my mother, despite everything."

I stared at the foam on my cocoa. A bad war. The coat. A moment of panic, then...no. Couldn't be. Caretakers aren't cashmere types.

"What about your family?" he said.

"Oh, well..." I scratched at a loose thread on one of the badges.

"I sense a reluctance to discuss."

"Nothing much to discuss." My biggest lie yet.

"Okay. Let me guess. Based on what I know—good-looking mother, good-looking car—I'm thinking your father is what? A doctor?"

He brought his head down low and turned his face up to mine so I couldn't avoid him. "Lawyer? Businessman?"

"Something like that," I said. My father had a cashmere coat and a sterling silver spoon with a crest on it. Not an unreasonable assumption.

"Hmm. Just vague enough to be intriguing. Any brothers?"

"No." I couldn't even fake that one. Ninety percent of what I knew about boys I'd learned from Eddie.

"Sisters?"

"Yup."

"How many?"

He wouldn't believe me. "A lot."

"Man, you're a tough interview. One mother, one father who may or may not be a businessman—leading me, of course, to assume he's a gangster of some type—no brothers (you're quite adamant about that, which for some reason I find suspicious too) and an indeterminate number of sisters. There's a story here, I'm sure of it."

I was giggling into my neck again and hating myself for it.

"I'm right, aren't I? Oh, wait." Eddie hopped up and disappeared into the kitchen. Turned up the radio. Ran back in. "I love this song. C'mon. Let's dance."

He took the cocoa out of my hand, put it on the table, pulled me up.

"No." I'd stopped giggling. I'd only ever danced with Sara.

"C'mon. You shy? No one's going to see. I'll close my eyes." He did, and then he moved my hands back and forth to the music, singing loudly, off-key, "*I wanna hold your ha-a-a-a-and. I wanna hold your hand.* C'mon! How can you not dance to the Beatles?"

"I can't."

"Anyone can dance. Even my dad—and he's a one-legged drunk. C'mon. The song's almost over."

"I can't. These—these shorts are too big."

I sat down. He let go of my hand.

"That's your problem?"

"Yes." No.

"Well, I can fix that." He rummaged through his pockets. "Coming from your side of the tracks, you may not be aware of this, but there are certain things the lowly handyman always has upon his person. A jackknife, a dog biscuit, in case Rover doesn't remember him from the last time he unclogged the drains, and…ah, here it is…the ever-popular all-purpose piece of string."

He took a little bundle of twine out of his pocket. He pulled me up, took my hands and held them out at my sides like I was going to perform a swan dive.

"This won't hurt a bit." He threaded the twine through my belt loops. He leaned his head over my shoulder to do the back ones, and his shirt touched one side of my face and then the other side as he followed it around. When he finished, he pulled the ends of the string back and forth until they were even. It made my hips wiggle.

"Well, look at that," he said. "Didn't know you could do the Twist. And what's this now?" He pulled the string from side to side. "Looks like the rumba to me. Who said you can't dance?"

The song ended, and he gave me a fake scowl. "You made me miss the whole thing." He pulled the string tight and tied it in a bow.

I started to sit down—relieved—but then "Let It Be Me" by Betty Everett came on. Eddie grabbed my hand again, and then I was up and his arm was around my back. No eighteen inches of safe space between us this time. It was a slow dance. He danced me around the coffee table and into the middle of the room. My legs were like logs, my hands sticky as raw pork chops.

"Oh. Um. Look." I bent away from him. "The rain's stopped. I better go."

He leaned in to look at me, to figure out what I was saying and why. I slipped my hand out of his. He was smiling but not really.

"I'll get my stuff," I said.

He took me home.

Eight

*EDDIEEDDIEEDDIE**EddieEddieEddieEddieEddieEddie.*

The sewing machine was driving me crazy. It kept chugging out his name, and I didn't want to be reminded of him or the way he drove the boat or crinkled his eyes when he laughed or did that thing with his face when I said I wanted to go. I didn't want to be reminded of how I'd made a fool of myself. I just wanted to forget the whole thing ever happened.

The phone rang. Mrs. Smees picked it up, huffed, sighed, slammed it back down.

"Dot. I need you to take these up to the reading room. *Now.*"

She shoved a stack of linen at me. "Tell Mr. Oliphant next time he decides to host a ladies' tea at the last goldarn minute to get his own girls to pick up the tablecloths. You've got better things to do than to be running around for him."

I had no idea where the reading room was. Somewhere upstairs, I figured. The man at the front desk would know.

I went to the main floor and started down the hall toward the foyer. Just as I got to the kitchen, a waitress—the redhead I'd seen the day I arrived—came around the corner from the other direction. Her face was turned away. She was talking to someone behind her.

"You're terrible!" Voice sliding up and down like a kazoo.

I dove behind a big metal dish cart and saw Eddie take her arm, whisper something in her ear. Her eyes went big, then small, and then she stepped into the kitchen, shaking her head and laughing.

"I'm not kidding, Janice!" But he clearly was. He waited until the door swung shut behind her before turning and heading into the dining room, still chuckling.

I couldn't help myself. I followed him in.

It was almost two o'clock. Only a few people were still there, sipping their tea, picking at their desserts. Eddie had his back to me. I didn't know where I was going or what I'd do when I got there, but I kept inching toward him, a puppy tailing its first squirrel.

He stopped to talk to a guest, and I hustled over to the buffet table like I had business there. I turned back just in time to see him step out the patio door. I waited for a count of five, then walked over to the window to see where he was going.

He was halfway down the stairs, shoulders in shadow, hair lit up like a proceed-with-caution light. He looked back as if someone had just called his name. I stepped away before he could see me and bumped into something.

A man howled. Chairs scraped. A dish clattered to the floor. People craned to look. I ticked around, slowly, slowly, teeth clenched, not wanting to find out what disaster I'd caused.

A man was standing behind me. His hands were out to his sides, and his mouth was wide open as if he'd just hit the final note of his opening number, but his eyes were nuts. Wisps of steam rose off his chest. His white shirt was drenched in coffee. We took each other in for a few seconds, then he went, "You. Why. You."

I couldn't move. A waitress raced over with a handful of napkins and blotted the man's shirt. Another man—tall, dark hair, blue-black shadow where his whiskers would be— was suddenly there too, patting his shoulder, telling him to calm down, telling the waitress everything was fine.

"What? Did you see her? Look!" the first man said, but the second one just shrugged.

"It's only coffee, Len. These things happen."

Mr. Oliphant bustled up, snapping his fingers at his staff. Someone appeared with a mop, and he huddled with the two men, whispering apologies about the new girl, not a waitress at all but a seamstress—didn't know why she was even here. He'd see that appropriate measures were taken to ensure this type of thing didn't occur again. He managed to say all that and still find time to shoot me a look over his shoulder that said, *Go somewhere and die.*

I scuttled away with the bundle of tablecloths in my arms and devastation on my face. The red-haired waitress was there now and doing her best to deal with both.

"Relax," she said. "That's Leonard Peters. He goes bananas all the time," and I didn't hate her quite so much for laughing with Eddie. She even promised to take the tablecloths to the reading room for me.

I went back downstairs and stood outside the housekeeper's office. I was going to lose my job. That's what Mr. Oliphant meant by appropriate measures. I could hear Mrs. Smees laughing inside. This was exactly the type of thing that would make her day.

I said a short prayer and pushed open the door. Eddie was sitting on a filing cabinet, folding a napkin into a swan and grinning.

"Dot. We've had a request for your services." Mrs. Smees almost smiled at me. "Miss Cameron has a sewing problem and asked to borrow you for the afternoon. Edward, here, promises to return you in the same condition I'm lending you in."

Eddie jumped off the filing cabinet and grabbed my arm. "Hurry," he said, "before the spell wears off," and Mrs. Smees actually laughed at that too.

Nine

WE CUT ACROSS the beach and behind some cabins, then turned onto Cameron Lane.

I waited for Eddie to make some comment about the dining room incident, but he didn't. He didn't mention Sunday either, so maybe (*maybe, maybe, please, maybe*) it wasn't that bad. He was his normal, cheery self.

"So who's this Miss Cameron?" I said, trying my best to sound normal too.

"Cameron Farm Equipment?"

I shook my head.

"You really aren't from around here, are you?"

"Nope."

"Well, here's everything you need to know about Buckminster. We've got lots of fancy guests who come for the summer, but there are only four families from town who count. The Camerons, who own the factory. The Adairs, who own the resort. The Andersons, who own the newspaper. And the McGuires."

"What do they own?"

"The still. They're the bootleggers." He waggled his eyebrows. "Those are our VIPs. Anyone else who lives in Buckminster is just a townie. Even Muriel accepts that. So when Miss Cameron needs mending done— or when the guy who looks after her property and takes her to the Arms for lunch twice a week thinks she needs mending done—Muriel is more than happy to make paid staff available."

"What does she need me to do?"

"I'm sure we'll find something."

Miss Cameron's cottage was called Birchdale, and looked like it would be full of ghosts or vampires or at least the type of butler who'd sprinkle arsenic on your crumpets if you weren't careful. It was a big brown wooden building three stories high, with a turret, stained-glass windows and a covered verandah. Some cottage.

I expected Miss Cameron to be one of those pretty young women I saw around the resort, who wore pearls even when they played tennis, but I was way off. Miss Cameron was the old lady in the turban I'd seen Eddie helping up the stairs the other day.

She was sitting in a wicker chair on the porch, a cat in her lap, an easel in front of her. I was close enough to see the brushstrokes on the picture she was painting before she noticed us.

"Eddie!" she said, or maybe *crowed* is a better word. Her voice was rough and cracked, but she smiled like a girl when she saw him. "What a marvelous surprise!"

I'd never seen anyone wear so much makeup. She looked like Cleopatra at eighty.

"You're painting roses?" he said.

She gave an elaborate shrug. "I know. Like an old lady. Can't get around anymore. I'm stuck painting whatever's at hand. Next thing I'll be doing portraits of the plumbing fixtures. Which, come to think of it, might not be a bad idea."

Eddie kissed her cheek and scratched her cat before introducing me. "I brought my friend Dot to see about that torn slipcover in the pink bedroom."

"Which pink bedroom?"

"Third floor? Toward the front?"

"That's pink now?" She slapped the side of her face. The sapphire in her ring was the size of a small potato. "Anything above the main floor is a foreign country to me these days. Well, why, sure. Go take a look. When you come back, though, mind getting me some"—she fiddled with an earring—"*tea*? Should be a bottle in the dining room if Frieda hasn't gone and hidden it again."

Miss Cameron raised her eyebrows. Eddie wagged his finger. She pouted. He sighed, then nodded. She smiled at me. "Isn't he adorable?"

"Don't feel obliged to respond," Eddie said. "Unless, of course, you can't help yourself."

The house was dark and full of old-fashioned furniture, but the walls were plastered with paintings. Some you'd expect in a place like this—pictures of bouquets and sailboats and cranky-looking old men with beards like cartoon explosions—but the others? Portraits with noses where foreheads should be, raggedy drawings of animal skeletons, great big pictures that looked like someone had splashed the paint on with a mop. I'd never seen anything like them.

"Wow," I said.

"I know," he said. "Wow."

"She did all these?"

"Most of them—except the old guys in the gold frames and some paintings by her students."

I stopped on the landing and looked at a portrait of a young girl who glared back as if she'd just caught me stealing.

"Guess who that is," Eddie said.

"Haven't a clue."

"Ida."

"*Ida?* From the cafeteria? Why would she paint Ida?"

"Miss Cameron used to give art lessons to local girls. Ida must have posed for her while she was here."

"Is Ida a good artist?"

He lowered his chin and looked at me. "You've had her meatloaf. What do you think the chances are?"

The paintings trailed off the higher up we went. By the third floor, the walls were almost bare. Eddie opened the door to a room in the turret and ushered me inside.

"I thought you said it was the pink bedroom."

He shrugged. "Close enough."

The room was definitely blue. Once upon a time, a little girl must have slept here. The bedspread was flounced, the wallpaper covered in lilies. A china doll sat straight-legged and blank-eyed on the dresser.

"There's something I want to talk to you about." Eddie sat on the bed and patted the coverlet like *sit down*.

I went red. He popped off the bed. "Oops. Sorry. Shouldn't have done that." Now he was red too. "The whole reason I brought you here was to say sorry. About yesterday. I didn't mean to scare you off."

I opened my mouth as if I might actually have a response.

"You don't have to say anything. I just wasn't sure you'd want to see me again, given, you know, the way things ended. I thought if Muriel ordered you to go and you had a chance to witness how nice I am to old people and animals, you'd, like..."

He tilted his head.

"I'd, like, what?"

"I don't know. Realize how perfectly respectable I can be when I'm on my best behavior."

I willed myself not to chew on my lip.

"You did notice how I was nice to old people and animals, didn't you?"

I shook my head, laughed a little.

"Oh, come on! I patted the cat. Kissed Miss Cameron. And as soon as we're done here, I intend to smuggle her bottle of rye past the World's Meanest Nurse."

"That's nice?"

"Sure is. You'd want a drink too if you had to live with the Hyena. She makes Muriel look like Tinker Bell." He was leaning against a little yellow dressing table, back in his element. "You don't believe me."

"Yeah, well, you thought I looked like Catwoman."

"I just calls 'em as I sees 'em."

"And a toad."

"I said you had toad-like qualities. There's a big difference. I also said how much I like toads. You just don't know a compliment when you hear one."

I walked over to the window, looked down on the big green yard and tried to give the impression I'd flirted with lots of guys. My heart thumped away like a crazy person hurling himself at a locked door.

"Okay then." Eddie clapped his hands. "So, what could you fix around here? Wouldn't want Muriel thinking I lured you away under false pretenses."

"Even though you did."

"'Specially because I did. And no doubt will again, given the opportunity."

I wandered around the room, picking up this and that, trying not to sweat out loud. "Nothing needs fixing that I can see." I flipped over a cushion. "The trim's a bit loose here, but not much I can do about that at the moment. I didn't bring my sewing stuff."

"I, however, am always prepared." He pulled a little sewing kit out of his pocket. "As you know, I'm a Scout."

He took my hand.

"And a perfect gentleman." He leaned down and kissed it, his lips dry, a little scratchy. "Or, at least, will make every attempt to be."

He picked a copy of *The Velveteen Rabbit* off the bookshelf and settled into the side chair. "Now I'm going to catch up on my reading while you get your work done."

I just needed my hand to stop shaking enough for me to thread the needle.

I fixed the cushion, and we headed downstairs. My job was to distract Frieda (who I would never have said resembled a hyena if Eddie hadn't pointed out the hunchy thing she did with her shoulders). I got her to look for an imaginary plaid blanket with a frayed edge while he figured out where she'd hidden Miss Cameron's rye. Judging by the gleam in their eyes when I got back, he'd found it.

Miss Cameron blew on her so-called tea before taking a sip, and they both laughed. "So, Lucinda," she said. "Manage to get everything straightened away?"

I looked behind me. Eddie rolled his eyes. "This is Dot, Miss Cameron."

"Dot! Goodness, that's nothing like Lucinda. Where'd I get the name Lucinda?"

Eddie elbowed her. "How many cups of tea have you had today?"

"Oh, you!" She looked at me now. "Beware, my dear. The Nicholson men are dangerous. This one's every bit as bad as his father. You'll fall in love with him if you're not careful."

I died.

Eddie said, "I'm not the least bit dangerous."

"No offense, darling! I've always had a thing for dangerous men. Now sit, you two. Tell me the gossip. I used to know everything that went on around these parts. Now I'm like some old hermit. What have you got that's juicy for me?"

Ten

EDDIE AND MISS Cameron yakked on about people
I didn't know—the Andersons, the Adairs, some of the
cottagers and her no-good nephew, who hadn't been back to
the lake more than five times since the war. I didn't mind.
She was funny. She made me promise I'd come by someday
to get my portrait painted, and then Frieda shooed us out.
It was time for Miss Cameron's medication.

Eddie borrowed Miss Cameron's boat, and we stopped
to check on one of "his" cottages. The owners were away
until the end of July. I helped him with the yardwork and
removing a swallow's nest from the dryer vent. By then it
was six, and we were hungry.

"I could take you back to the Arms, and you might get
the last serving of Ida's tuna casserole, or I could make you
dinner at my place," he said. "Your choice."

"You a good cook?"

"No. But neither is Ida, and I'm cuter."

I wobbled my hand back and forth, surprised at myself.

He ignored my attempt at humor, and we headed across the lake to his cottage. It was a beautiful, calm evening, so we decided to eat on the deck. Eddie fired up the barbecue.

"Burgers okay? They're kinda my specialty."

I said, "Sure," but when he came back out of the cottage, he had a half-empty package of hot dogs in his hand and a sheepish look on his face.

"Sorry. Pop must have been around. All I've got left is five hot dogs and half a loaf of raisin bread."

"Sounds good to me."

"Good?"

"Okay. Interesting."

"I can work with interesting."

That's all there was to dinner—hot dogs on raisin bread and the Kool-Aid I made by chipping rock-hard sugar out of an old glass jar—but it managed to last until eleven o'clock. We just kept talking.

His mother's name was Dorcas (a family name). I told him my mother's name was Joyce, but only because he asked and that is Mrs. Welsh's name.

The best thing that ever happened to him was his uncle letting him drive the car when he was ten. The best thing that ever happened to me was happening right that second, but I didn't say that. I said it was the first time I went into town with my sisters for an ice cream.

"So what's the worst thing that ever happened to you?" I said before he could ask for details.

"Easy. I was getting my tonsils out and woke up halfway through the operation with the doctor's hands down my throat. They hadn't given me enough anesthetic. To make it even worse, it was my fifth birthday."

"When's your birthday?" I said.

"I tell you this heartbreaking story and all you can say is *when's your birthday?*"

"You were the one who said it happened on your birthday. It seemed impolite not to ask."

"Fine. August 26. When's yours?"

I wanted to lie, but I couldn't come up with a single other plausible date, even with the hundreds I had to choose from. He discombobulated me.

"July 8."

"That's a week Wednesday."

"Oh? Really? I kind of forgot all about it." Ha. Hardly.

"They're having a party behind the colony that night. We should go. Or we could do something special, just the two of us, if you prefer."

I felt my face getting hot again, and he spared me by saying, "Okay. Your turn. What's the worst thing that ever happened to you?"

I told him about our home burning down—but not *the* Home, just a home, a long time ago. I told him what it smelled like, how loud it was with the flames roaring and walls collapsing and my "sisters" crying and screaming and how, even over all that, I could hear my own breath and my own heart.

He said I should be a writer and took another shriveled hot dog off the grill—cold now—and ate it like a limp carrot stick. "That's what I want to be. A writer."

"You already are," I said.

"A two-column article on the Buckminster stamp show is not writing."

"It's a start."

He nodded like, *Yeah, okay, but* and began to talk about politics and world leaders and making a difference. That type of writing. He wasn't his usual twinkly self, but I could tell this made him happy.

Somewhere along the line I realized I could barely see him anymore, just those teeth and his white T-shirt. It was dark and we'd missed the sunset and I hadn't even noticed.

Early in the evening he'd propped a radio on the picnic table and fiddled with the antenna until he picked up a signal. Now that Beatles song came on again, his favorite one. This time I would have danced, but he went, "Yikes" and squinted to make out the time on his watch. "You've missed curfew."

I didn't even know I had a curfew. We hurried to the boat, then skipped across the calm surface of the lake. He drove past Miss Cameron's, past the lodge and the little guest cabins along the shore. I thought he'd gone too far, but then he turned off the engine, and we glided into the next dock.

"My best customers," he said, getting out of the boat. "They won't mind. We'll slip in the back way so you don't get caught."

He put his finger to his lips when we passed a cabin near the dock—the guy was apparently a light sleeper—and then we cut across a steep lawn to the woods.

He took my hand and led me down a path I couldn't see. Everything was that floaty gray color of dreams. He helped me over fallen trees, held back branches and got me to the edge of the Feudal Colony.

"Know your way from here?"

He was going to let go of my hand.

"Yeah. I'm just over there. In the seamstress's cabin. The little one behind the bushes. But you know that. So. Anyway."

"Okay. Good." He paused. "Listen. This might not be appropriate, but—"

I swallowed. I hoped my lips weren't chapped, that I didn't have raisins between my teeth, that I'd just naturally figure out how to do this.

"I could use a hand if you ever want to help out with my cottages again. I know you're busy and everything, so—"

"No. No. Sure. That would be wonderful. I mean, fabulous." Way too enthusiastic. Crazy-lady enthusiastic.

"Great. I'll be in touch."

"In touch."

"Yes. In touch."

There was probably something I was supposed to do at that point—some signal, some code—but I didn't know what it was, so I said, "Thank you" and he said, "You're welcome," like it was a joke, and that seemed to be the end, so I said bye and he said bye and I let go of his hand and walked into the Feudal Colony alone.

I turned around to wave, but I couldn't tell if he was gone or not. I ran back to my cabin as if Sara was there and waiting to hear all about it.

Eleven

I **WAS ALMOST** back to my cabin when Glennie stepped out of the Harem. The light above the door made her curlers sparkle. She had a pink cosmetic kit, slightly smaller than your average hockey bag, tucked under her arm.

"Oh, hey!" she said, bouncing over. "I've been thinking about you. What's your name again?"

"Dot."

"Right. Dot. I realize forgetting your name makes me sound somewhat insincere about wanting to see you—but banish that thought. Just the way I am. Slightly scatterbrained. All part of my enormous charm." She took a bobby pin out of her hair and opened it with her teeth. "So what have you been up to?"

And because she was there and Sara wasn't, I said, "I've been out with Eddie Nicholson."

"I heard that from one of the dock boys—and he wasn't too thrilled about it, I must say. Too bad. If Finlay wanted you, he should've moved faster. I told him that." She rammed the bobby pin through a curler, almost dropping her cosmetic bag in the process. "Isn't Eddie a charmer?"

My shoulders squeezed into my neck with the utter thrill of it. "Yes."

"Did he take you for lunch in Hidden Bay?"

I nodded.

"In some swish boat?"

"Really nice boat."

"Probably Ward's. And then back to that cottage of his?"

I nodded again.

"Isn't it appalling? But what can you do? *Maman est disparue* and papa as good as. But you no doubt heard all about that. Gunky's 'bad' war, the leg blown to smithereens at—insert name of battle here—the subsequent drinking…"

"Gunky?" I said. "That's his father's name?"

"That's what they call him. Must be short for Gordon or Gunga Din or something. I don't know. Anyway"—she flapped a hand in front of her like a puppy begging—"that's not what I wanted to talk to you about. I've been terrible, ignoring you like this. High time you got to know some of the youngsters around here—so I'm taking you to the Bye-Bye Baby party. And PS, Finlay will be there."

"Who's Finlay?"

"Finlay? Finlay Hart. The dock boy I told you about. Black hair. Imposing physique. Old money. He was ogling you from the dock today. You didn't notice?"

"No."

"Oh, he'll be livid. Finlay is used to being noticed. So—
Bye-Bye Baby? You're on?"

"Ahh. When is it?" I'd never been to a party before.

"The Wednesday after next. Be there or be square, as
they say."

This was the party Eddie'd been talking about. I didn't
want to go. Not with all those strangers. It made me feel
slightly sick. "I've got a lot of work to do. Mrs. Smees
doesn't—"

"You clearly don't know what Bye-Bye Baby is."

I put on an awkward semi-smile while I tried to come
up with an answer.

"I knew it. Bye-Bye Baby—Triple B, if you will—is the
annual commemoration of a bizarre occurrence that took
place right here seventeen years ago."

She looped her arm through mine. "Picture this. A girl
and a boy. In the woods. After curfew. Doing the type of
things hot-blooded teens are known to do after curfew.
At some point in the proceedings, they come up for air, only
to discover a baby. Lying on the ground." She paused for
effect. "A tiny, blood-soaked newborn baby." She held up her
hand. "No bigger than this."

My jaw fell. My eyes popped.

"Oooh. What a gratifying reaction."

"What happened to the baby?"

"That's the thing. That's why July 8, 1947, shall live on in
infamy. The couple was understandably concerned to find
a defenseless infant left in the woods. I mean, who knows

what could have happened? A wild animal could have raised it as its own. One of the guests' Yorkies could have trotted down to the patio with its tiny lifeless body clamped between its jaws. You can imagine how terrible that would be for business. So, being good Dunbrae employees, they attempted to rescue the child. They reached over to pick it up and—poof!"

I jumped.

"The baby disappeared right before their eyes. Now we honor this momentous occasion every year by returning to that very same spot and doing what those employees did so long ago: drinking ourselves stupid. I'd hate for you to miss it."

She went on for a while in that same vein, then must have headed to the staff washroom. I don't remember. I stood alone in the courtyard of the colony, my head buzzing.

An unusually tiny baby.

Born the very day I was born.

The mysterious disappearance.

The coat.

The Buckminster address.

I stumbled back to my cabin in a fog. I stood on the step to unlock the door and something crunched beneath my shoe. I flicked it away with my foot, figuring it was just a twig. I was too rattled by Glennie's story to check.

I realize now, of course, it was probably the first of the bones.

Twelve

"WHAT'S THIS?"

Mrs. Smees spilled a pile of floral silk onto my table, then stood back, arms crossed, squinting at me.

"That's Mrs. Illsley's dress. I—"

"I know what it is. I just don't know why you'd call it fixed." She pulled a pencil out of her hair and poked at the dress. "That seam look fixed to you? Think that's enough to keep them big hips of hers from busting out all over the family pew when she kneels down at St. Ninian's this Sunday?"

"Oh. No, I must have just missed it. I—"

"Missed? I'm not paying you to *miss* things. My guess is you're spending more time thinking about our young Mr. Nicholson than you are about your job."

She was only partly right about Eddie. I'd barely slept the night before. I couldn't get that story about the baby out of my head.

It couldn't have been true. It was just a creepy story. A creepy made-up story like the ones Patsy used to tell us about the ghost of Mrs. Hazelton's dead (and usually naked) lover roaming the halls of the Home every full moon and calling, calling, calling her name. We'd all scream and huddle together and make someone come to the bathroom with us for weeks afterward, despite knowing full well she'd concocted the whole thing. (Mrs. Hazelton with a lover? Even I couldn't swallow that one.)

This was the same. I knew the story had to be nonsense, but I still couldn't shake it. I'd tossed and turned all night, trying to make sense of it. All these years fantasizing about where I'd come from, I'd never considered anything mystical about my background. The parents I'd dreamed up may have been implausible, but they'd always been human.

Now two tiny babies, two mysteries, same date, both linked to Buckminster. Hard not to entertain the idea that there was some connection. The disappearing-before-their-very-eyes thing just kind of ruled out a human one. I wondered if the ladies' auxiliary was going to tell me the spoon came from a witch's coven or something.

I had another go at Mrs. Illsley's dress and was careful to make sure everything was perfect this time. I just prayed Mr. Oliphant would hold off telling Mrs. Smees about the coffee incident until I was back in her good books again. I didn't need two strikes against me.

I ate a sandwich at my table at lunchtime and didn't take a break until Mrs. Smees said, "It's quarter to six.

Get going. Don't hang around here, expecting me to pay you overtime."

By the time I got to the colony, other kids were already there. Dock boys shooting their balled-up Dunbrae shirts into a hoop nailed to the side of the Meat Department, waitresses laughing and whispering on the steps of the Harem. I didn't want to run into them. I slid in along the hedge to my cabin, then jumped back, hand over mouth.

Eddie was sitting on the steps behind the lilac bushes.

"You. Scared. Me."

"Sorry. Didn't mean to—which isn't to say I didn't enjoy it immensely."

"Did I do that toad thing again?"

"Toad? You? I have no idea of what you speak." He patted the steps and slid over to make room next to him.

"What's that in your hand?" I said.

He shrugged. "The remains of a bird, by the looks of it." He tossed the bones into the bushes. "So, can I drag you out tonight? Take you to the falls maybe. You like fishing?"

"Yeah, I do. I'd really love to, but—" I couldn't screw up at work again. I couldn't lose my job. "I think I should just go to bed. Mrs. Smees got mad at me today."

"That's news?"

"Well, yeah. This time I deserved it. I was sloppy. Too tired, I guess. Didn't sleep well last night."

He leaned down and pulled my foot onto his knee. "How come?" He tied my shoe for me, then put it back down.

"Bad dreams," I managed to say.

"Smees dreams?"

"No. I ran into Glennie after you took me home. She told me this ghost story, and I don't know, it just kind of spooked me."

"Excellent. I love ghost stories. Unburden yourself." He bumped elbows with me, and the hairs on my arm all reached out for him. "Tell me."

"You probably know it already. Bye-Bye Baby? Silly."

"That's not a ghost story. That actually happened."

I looked at him out of the corner of my eye.

"I'm not kidding." He raised his hand. "Scout's honor."

"A baby disappeared into thin air?"

"Well, okay. That part's made up, but the rest is true."

"How do you know? You wouldn't have been around. You're too young."

"My babysitter."

"You have a babysitter? Big boy like you?"

The elbow again. "When I was a kid, I mean. After Mum left. Dad needed someone to look after me while he was working. This college girl helped out. Sandra Smithers. She's Conway now. Anyway, I heard her talking about the Bye-Bye Baby party one day with her friends—this would have been five or six years later, I guess—and I asked her what it was. That was the great thing about Sandra. You were cute enough, she'd tell you anything."

"And? What'd she say?"

He leaned back, his elbows on the step behind him, legs out straight like hockey sticks. Deck shoes. No socks.

"I thought you were tired," he said.

"Not that tired."

"Okay. Well. That area back there?" He leaned around the lilac bush and pointed to the woods beyond the colony. "I mean, way back. Good ten-, fifteen-minute walk. There's a clearing. Kids have had their parties there forever. Dad said they even did in his day. Anyway, that night a bunch of kids go up as per usual. Somewhere toward midnight, this couple goes off on their own and they hear a noise. At first they think it's an animal. Maybe it's been hurt or something, so they go to look and find this, like, minuscule baby just lying on the ground."

"That's pretty much what Glennie told me."

"Yeah. But here's where it gets different. Story they tell now is that the baby vanished before their very eyes, right? *Ripley's Believe It or Not!* stuff. That's not what Sandra said. She said the kids left the baby to get help. She was the first person they found, so the three of them raced back. By the time they got there, the baby was gone. Someone had taken it."

"Taken it?"

"Yeah."

"Who?"

"Beats me."

"Where was the mother?"

He shrugged. "No sign of anyone. No one's ever figured out how it got there."

"What happened to the baby?"

"Ditto. No clue. Mention it now and everyone acts like it's a myth or something. As if you're asking what happened to Snow White or the tooth fairy."

We sat on the steps, quiet for a while. Me thinking— more like *believing* in that you-just-know kind of way—that this was my story. That there might actually be a rational explanation after all. I didn't know what the explanation was yet, of course, or how I was going to go about finding it.

And then suddenly, I just did.

"You should do a story on it," I said. "For the paper."

Eddie turned and looked at me. "I was thinking the exact same thing."

"Eerie, isn't it?" Our little joke, but he didn't laugh.

"It is." He was sitting up now, kind of twitchy through the shoulders, eyes sparkly. "Make a great article. Everyone around here has heard the rumors. Maybe it's time the real story came out."

"Where are you going to get that?"

He rolled out his bottom lip and thought. "So this happened in 1948…"

"In '47. At least, according to Glennie."

"Right—'47. The *Gleaner* may have done something on it then, though not if it just looked like a bunch of kids making up stories. Still, there might be some clues there. I'll check the office, see if they have issues going back that far. There's also the resort's reading room."

"What is that anyway? Mrs. Smees wanted me to go there the other day."

"It's like a library. Books, magazines, that type of thing, but they also keep photos and newspaper clippings about anything connected to the Arms."

"Such as?"

"I don't know. Weddings, funerals, obits, not to mention endless stories about dock boys getting accepted at Yale or Mrs. So-and-So the Third hosting her much-anticipated annual garden party. Could be something there."

He put his hands behind his neck, looked at the sky, then shook his head. "You know what though? I doubt it. A missing baby? Not the type of story the Arms likes to remember. They'd be more likely to cover it up. Not sure where else to look."

"What about your babysitter? She still around?"

He gawked at me. I thought I'd said something wrong.

"Sandra. Of course. I even ran into her last week. She asked if I'd pop by her cottage. She's got some sort of rodent problem. Want to come—or you too tired?"

He laughed when I said no girl could resist a boy with a rodent problem.

Thirteen

I CHANGED OUT of my uniform and tried to make myself adorable or at least presentable while Eddie waited outside. Next payday, I was splurging on some barrettes.

A bunch of kids were hanging around outside the Meat Department when we left. A dark-haired guy sitting on the roof of a truck, pants rolled up to the knees, bare feet bouncing off the window, went, "Hey, Nicholson! What're you doing here? Someone's toilet clogged?"

"Not unless you've been at it again, Finlay." Eddie smiled like it was a big joke but whispered, "Jerk" as soon as he'd turned his back.

Glennie clearly had no idea what I was like if she thought *that* guy was my type. "No kidding," I said.

Instead of going down to the lake through the resort, we took the path behind the guest cabins and came out on the same property as the night before. It looked different in daylight. Last time, I'd only noticed the little cottage by the water. Now I saw there was a big house up on the hill too.

"Since we're at the Adairs', mind if I take a quick measurement?" Eddie said. "Ward wants me to fix a screen for him."

I didn't mind anything he did.

We went around to the back of the big house. Eddie felt above the window until he found the key and opened the door.

"C'mon in."

To the Adairs'? No way. These were the people who owned the resort.

"C'mon. Nothing to worry about. They're not here. And they wouldn't care anyway. C'mon."

I followed him through the kitchen to the—I don't know—conservatory? Big old wingback chairs with chintz slipcovers gone chalky at the arms. Striped curtains faded to beige and beiger. Lots of books and photos and prehistoric plants. The type of room where you'd kill Colonel Mustard with a candlestick.

"You know what I don't get?" I said.

"Hold this." Eddie took a piece of paper and a pencil out of his pocket and handed them to me. "What?"

"Why it's taken seventeen years for someone to look into this."

He stretched up to measure the window. "Forty-eight inches. Write that down, would you?"

"I mean, a little baby. In the forest. Animals. Bugs. Something terrible could have happened to her."

"Her?"

"What?"

"You said *her*. You know something I don't?"

Goose bumps bubbling up like hives. "No. I mean him, her, it...I don't know." A laugh so phony Eddie actually turned and squinted at me. "It just doesn't seem right."

He took one last measurement and put his tape away. "Maybe people knew the mother and were protecting her. Or maybe someone told them to keep their mouths shut."

"Like who?"

He leaned against the wall, opened his hand as if he'd just tossed a ball up into the air. "The baby's father? The mother's father maybe?"

"The jilted husband?"

"An affair? Oooh. That'll get the *Gleaner* flying off the stands." He stepped back and smoothed the curtains. "Might even have been someone from the Arms. An employee messing around with a guest. Lots of people wouldn't have wanted a scandal like that getting out."

But someone had left that coat and spoon at the Home. There'd been someone who didn't want it hidden entirely. That's what Mrs. Hazelton had said.

And that's what I almost said myself. I took a breath, opened my mouth, then froze.

"Ye-es?" Eddie leaned forward like, *This is going to be good.*

I had no way of knowing for sure if I was the baby. Eddie didn't know I was an orphan. And anyway, who knew what the guy had been thinking, leaving that stuff at the Home?

"Nothing," I said. "Just thought I was going to sneeze."

ce

No fancy cruiser that day. This time it was an old tin boat— Eddie's own—with a little motor on the back and water sloshing in the bottom.

Sandra's cottage was on a tiny island called Laffalot, or at least that's what was written in drippy blue house paint on the diving rock out front. Eddie had barely gotten the boat tied up when a little girl in a baggy pink bathing suit threw herself into his arms.

"Shouldn't you be getting ready for bed?"

"Mum said we could have a swim first."

"Where is she?"

"On the patio. But she's not going to be very happy you're here."

"What'd I do this time?"

"You'll see." She wriggled out of his arms, took his hand and pulled him toward the cottage.

Sandra was sitting in the shade, smoking a cigarette and flipping through a dog-eared copy of *Lady's Circle*. She had a towel around her shoulders and blue goop in her hair.

She covered her face and shrieked when she saw us. "Jody! Mummy said no visitors!"

Eddie cracked up. "And here I always took you for a natural blond, Sandra."

She swatted him a little harder than was absolutely necessary. "I don't care about you, but your friend here didn't need to know all my intimate secrets."

"Relax. Dot's like a Russian spy. Wouldn't talk under torture."

Sandra settled back in her lawn chair and found her cigarette. "So. You here about our plague of rodents?"

"Thursday. I promise. I'll do it when you take the kids to swimming. Today I want to talk to you about a professional matter."

She turned up her chin and aimed a tight rod of smoke at the wind chimes dangling from the eaves. "Oooh, my. A professional matter. And to think I used to wipe your little bottom. Do tell."

"I'm writing a story for the *Gleaner* on Bye-Bye Baby."

"Talking to the wrong person, I'm afraid. I haven't been to the party in years."

"No. The real Bye-Bye Baby. What actually happened."

Her face changed. Went longer, thinner, kind of blank. A mug shot. She leaned back in her chair, arm bent up at the elbow, thumb flicking at her cigarette filter.

"Why open that can of worms twenty years after the fact?"

"Seventeen. And why are you calling it a can of worms?" If Sandra was hoping to turn Eddie off the story, she'd said the wrong thing.

"Jody," she said, "go find your sister. You can play for fifteen minutes. Then it's lights-out."

She waited until the little girl had crawled all over Eddie, found his Life Savers and skipped off before she said anything else. "I doubt I'll be much help."

"You know more than most people. You were there."

"Yes. But that was a long time ago, and I was"—she ran her tongue under her upper lip—"indisposed. I also don't want to get anyone in trouble."

"Like who?"

"Don't know. But someone out there'd be none too pleased to see this story rearing its ugly head again."

He smiled at her.

"Don't waste your time, Eddie. I don't fall for that type of thing from you anymore—Jody! Quit hogging the Slinky! It's Wendy's turn."

"A little baby, left in the woods. Must be hard for a mother to hear something like that," Eddie said.

Sandra wasn't stupid. She stared at Eddie until she'd made it very clear she knew exactly what he was up to, then tapped the ashes off her cigarette and almost nodded. "May as well sit down then. Grab a chair for your friend there."

"You're the best."

"Don't use my name. I don't want this coming back to bite me. Last thing I need, stuck here all summer, is to get cut off anyone's guest list."

Eddie solemnly swore not to use her name, then fished out a scrap of paper and a pencil. "So shoot. What happened?"

She didn't answer right away. She sipped her drink. Wiped a little of the hair goop off her leg. Sighed. "Okay. It was a Tuesday, which was unusual because we never went to the clearing on Tuesdays—we went to the dance at the Boat Club. But this week some idiot had pulled a fire alarm, and the manager kicked us all out. Not much else to do around here ten o'clock on a weeknight, so some of us went to the clearing."

"How many of you?"

"I'd say ten, twelve girls and maybe a few more boys than that. We all worked at the Arms. The girls were cottagers or university students, but some of the boys were townies. We all hung out together, especially when nobody else was watching."

Eddie smiled at that. "And, of course, nobody was watching at the clearing."

"Exactly. Anyway, someone had gotten their hands on some gin, and things were getting pretty wild. I seem to remember there was a fight. Usually was—or at least a bit of pushing around. Never amounted to much. Just a chance for the boys to flex their biceps for the girls. A few kids had gotten sick and left. Couples had started pairing off. I had this thing for a townie named Dougie Pratt, but he'd disappeared with Cecily Ingram—who, up to that point,

I'd figured for my best friend—so I was sitting by the camp-fire, plotting revenge."

"Not like you," Eddie said.

"You'd be surprised. Anyway, around midnight I heard Cecily come out of the woods crying, and let me tell you, I couldn't have been more delighted. I figured Dougie had resisted her advances. That's the only reason I went over—to gloat—but I couldn't make out a word she was saying. It took me a while to realize she wasn't wailing about Dougie. She was wailing about some baby they'd found. Sounded like the booze talking, but next thing Dougie stag-gered out of the woods too. He was nodding at everything Cecily said, eyes all bulged out, and I started to think there was something to this. So I said, *Where? Where's the baby?* But then they suddenly didn't want to tell me. Started jabbering about how they were going to get in trouble or what if their boss found out or their parents. You'd think they'd *had* the baby, not found it."

"Could that be what happened?" Eddie stopped scrib-bling. "Cecily had the baby and the story was just a cover-up?"

Sandra took another pull on her cigarette. She shook her head, blew smoke out the side of her mouth. "I don't care how tiny that baby was. There's no way Cecily was pregnant. I saw her in her underwear on a daily basis. She had a waist about the circumference of a lightbulb. I always figured she'd had a few ribs removed. Wouldn't put it past her."

"What were they so afraid of then?" I said.

"For starters, no one was supposed to go up in the woods *anyway*—and these kids were seventeen and blind drunk on bootlegged liquor. That alone was a hanging offense. Big thing, though, was that Dougie was a townie and Cecily was an Ingram. She was no doubt thinking, 'Mother will skin me alive if she finds out I've been with a Pratt.' I imagine Dougie was worried too. Back then, there were rules about dating other employees. People might have turned a blind eye if Cecily and Dr. Talbot's boy got together, but Dougie knew he'd lose his job if Mrs. Ingram found out about the two of them."

That surprised me. "It was that bad?"

Both Eddie and Sandra laughed.

"But why did anyone even need to know they were together?" Eddie said. "They could have just made up some story."

"Yeah. Maybe. But we're back to where we started then, aren't we? They didn't want to be sounding the alarm with booze on their breath. They'd get in enough trouble about that as it was."

Eddie rocked his head like, *Well, okay.*

"Hey. I'm not saying it was right. That's just the way things were. Anyway. I convinced them we had to get the baby. Some nights it's dark as peat up there, but that night we barely needed a flashlight. Not a full moon but almost. They took me to that tree. You must know the one." She looked at Eddie. "Old maple or something, big vee in the middle."

He nodded, then turned to me. "It's kind of a landmark. Just past the clearing. There's this rock ledge beside it that almost makes a wall, so if you wanted some alone time, that's where you'd go."

Sandra waggled an eyebrow. "Unless somebody got there first, of course."

"Then you'd go to the pit," Eddie said.

"Good Lord. The pit. I forgot about that. You're right. There was the tree or the pit."

"Can get a little crowded back there with all the summer romances." Eddie looked at me, then looked away, and my face went hot as a slap.

"Yeah. So they took me to the tree—but the baby was gone. Couldn't have been more than five minutes from the time they told me till the time I got there." She paused. "Someone had taken it."

Eddie lifted his chin and scratched his neck. "You see anyone?"

"Nope. Maybe heard a bit of noise from the kids still in the clearing but didn't see a soul."

He gave a slow nod, lips scrunched up.

"You don't believe me?" Sandra said.

He lifted his hands in surrender. "It's not me. Tell me the sky's green, Sandra, and I'd believe you—but my editor? A couple of drunk kids claim to see a baby in the woods. It's gone when they come back, *therefore* someone stole it? He's not going to buy that. He'll say someone just fabricated the whole thing."

Sandra crushed her cigarette in the ashtray. "There was a baby and someone took it. I know that for sure."

"Like I say, I believe you. But got any proof?"

"Not anymore I don't—but I did." Triumphant.

"Yeah?" Eddie was trying not to smile.

"Listen. Half the reason I wanted them to show me the baby was because I didn't believe them. So when we got to the spot and there was nothing there, I just shrugged. Cecily was going on and on about how tiny it was, how maybe we just couldn't see it or were looking in the wrong place. Dougie was saying, *No, no, it was wrapped in a man's shirt and it was right here by the tree, next to the heart-shaped rock*...etcetera, etcetera. They were all in a tizzy, so I went through the motions, like I was looking for it too. Down on my hands and knees, patting the ground like I'd lost an earring. Then I hit something wet and sort of jumped back. Dougie went, *What?* I figured it was just a boggy part or something, but he swung his lighter around to see, and I lifted my hands and realized it wasn't mud. It was blood. My hands were covered in blood."

I felt faint. "Where would blood have come from?"

"Don't mean to scare you, dear, but Mother Nature doesn't make it easy for us gals." She looked at me with something like pity. "Giving birth is a bloody business."

Eddie was holding his mouth like he was trying to crack a nut between his teeth, like he still wasn't sure about all this.

"I apologize for washing my hands, Eddie," Sandra said. "Didn't realize I'd be required to provide proof seventeen years later."

"I'm just trying to see it from Mr. Quigley's perspective, that's all. He's going to say, *How do you know it wasn't a baby animal, or that some teenaged hooligan didn't just cut himself?* You know what he's like. Stickler for details."

Sandra was getting huffy. "Okay. Number one. Dougie told me they unwrapped the shirt, saw the umbilical cord, counted all the little fingers and toes. I don't know any animals with fingers, do you?"

I almost said, *Raccoon*, but I kept my mouth shut. *Our Forest Friends* used to be one of my favorite books too.

"And number two. If they'd just concocted some crazy story, they'd have gotten over it. But they didn't. Cecily changed that night. Stopped having fun—stopped *being* fun. Dougie quit the Arms, left town—and he wouldn't have done that lightly. His family needed the money."

That was good enough for me. "So what do you think happened to the baby then?"

Sandra looked across the lake, eyes fixed, not quite shaking her head. "Somehow, someone managed to sneak it out past twenty kids. To where? Don't know. I always wondered if there's a shallow grave up there that we missed."

"What about the mother?" I said. "Any sign of her?"

"Other than the blood? Not that we could see. We told the other kids there that night about the baby. Everyone turned on their lighters and flashlights and tromped through the woods, but there was nothing. That was another reason we all agreed not to tell. We'd just be getting ourselves into trouble for no good reason."

I said, "Any idea who the mother might have been?"

"No idea. And believe me, Cecily and I spent every waking moment that summer trying to figure that out."

"Any top contenders?"

"Oh, sure. Angela Landry—but it turned out she'd just put on a few pounds. That's a problem when you work as a waitress. Hard to keep your fingers out of the pastry tray. There were some other girls we wondered about too. Marcia Shaw, for instance, but that was based entirely on the fact we didn't like her. Our best lead was this other girl, a townie, who spent the summer in a big clown costume, entertaining the little kids. We figured she'd at least be able to hide the fact she was pregnant. She quit just after the baby was born, so we were all abuzz about her for a while, but then we found out she had mono. The manager got rid of her quick. All the Arms needed was a break-out of 'the kissing disease.' Can you imagine? They'd lose half their staff. Anyway, after a while we just gave up. We realized we'd probably never know who the mother was. Guests. New ones coming and going every week. Could have been anybody."

"What about the father?" My voice went funny just saying the word.

Sandra coughed out a laugh. "Think it's hard narrowing down the mother? The father could have been a teenage boy or a married man or someone's grandfather, for that matter."

"He might never have stepped foot in Buckminster County," Eddie said, "and even if he did, he'd have had nine months to disappear. No way of knowing who he was."

But there was.

I wanted to say something, but it was like when I was learning to skip. The rope would turn and I'd get ready to leap in, but then it would turn again, and again, and I'd still just be rocking on my toes, too afraid to jump in.

I decided I'd wait until I'd had a chance to talk to someone at St. Ninian's about the spoon before I said anything. I told myself I didn't want to explain everything in front of Sandra, but the truth was, I was just chicken.

"Where's she now?" Eddie asked.

"Who? Cecily?" Sandra's lips turned down, a frosted pink horseshoe. "Haven't the faintest. Wasn't someone I kept up with. Her parents divorced, sold the cottage. I don't think I saw her after that summer. She wasn't anxious to return."

"And Dougie?"

"He's in Toronto. Got a big job with a bank, I understand. Did okay for a little guy from Buckminster."

"He ever come back this way?"

"I saw him at his mother's funeral a few years ago but not since then. She used to clean for our family. Nice lady."

"What about other people who were there that night?" I asked.

"Oh, heavens." She lit another cigarette. "Carole Ferguson. Ann Cowan. Barney Someone-or-other..."

"Anyone who'd be here now?"

"Now? Like today?"

"Well, soon," Eddie said. "I'd like to get the article written before this year's party."

"I'll have to think about it." She noticed her watch. "Oh my Lord, Eddie! My hair! I was supposed to wash this out fifteen minutes ago. If I go bald…Girls, get Mummy's shampoo!"

She raced down to the dock and dove into the water, cigarette and all.

Fourteen

"**WHAT ARE YOU** thinking? Got enough for a story?"

I was supposed to get an early night so I'd be sharp for work the next day, but it didn't happen. We put the kids to bed while Sandra inspected her scalp for bald spots, then headed over to Eddie's for bologna and more raisin bread. (He promised he'd go grocery shopping before he asked me for dinner again.)

The day had cooled off suddenly—a north wind would do that, he said—so we were back inside, sitting on that old chesterfield.

"No. I need more proof than what Sandra's giving us. I might go into town tomorrow and talk to Dr. Talbot, poke around the hospital. See if anyone there remembers a woman showing up needing help."

"Seventeen years ago?"

"I know. Not likely. And even if someone did, doctors aren't allowed to blab about their patients' sordid little secrets. Sure make my job a lot easier if they were."

"Yeah, but then everyone would know about those extra toes of yours."

He flicked a raisin at me. "And what your nose used to look like."

"Ha."

"Ha yourself."

Eddie slid down into the cushions and chucked his crust into the fireplace. "I'm starting to think this story is a dead end. Too much time has passed. Too many maybe's, what-if's, could-be's, who-the-hell-knows. Sandra won't even let me use her name. I think I'm just going to drop it."

"No." My hand was on his somehow. "Don't do that. It's a really good story. I'd read it. Everyone would. Go to the hospital. Ask in town. Maybe Sandra will remember something else, someone else who might have been there."

He was smiling now. "Gee, I had no idea you were so keen."

I'd overdone it. My face went hot and I sank into my corner of the chesterfield, but he had my hand, and he wasn't letting go.

"Wanna help me with it?"

"Yes," I said.

"You want to?"

"I do."

"You really want to."

"Yes."

He laughed, but it was just low, and he was kind of biting his lip too. "Want to what?"

And I turned my face away.

"I'm embarrassing you."

"Yes."

"I'll stop."

I didn't really want him to, but I didn't know how to tell him that, so I didn't say anything, and he stopped, but before he did he looked at me a certain way, and that was almost more than I could stand anyway.

Fifteen

THE NEXT DAY started out like the best day of my life.

Ida made sticky buns and saved a big one for me.

On my way to the lodge, I ran into Miss Cameron, who still couldn't remember my name ("Close as I can get is that you're *not* Lucinda") but did refer to Eddie as my boyfriend ("Tell your boyfriend I've got bats again").

Then I got to work and there was a note on my table saying Mrs. Smees wouldn't be in until eleven. Bas must have known she'd be out because he had the radio turned up high. First song I heard was the Beatles singing "I Want To Hold Your Hand."

EddieEddieEddieEddieEddieEddieEddie.

I reached for the mending pile and pulled off the jacket on top. It was a girl's windbreaker, about my size, light blue. I checked the tag to see what needed fixing.

*I found this at the cottage and thought it would look good on
you. You'll need it for tonight. We're going fishing. Come over to
the Adairs' as soon as you're through work.*

Eddie.

*P.S. I called the editor last night. He gave me the go-ahead
on the Bye-Bye Baby story. Or should I say "us"?*

I looked around to make sure no one in the empty room
was watching, tore off the note and tucked it into my bra.
Someday I was going to have so much to tell Sara.

Mrs. Smees arrived at quarter to eleven. I was halfway
through a tricky bit on a sleeve so didn't look up until she
was at her desk.

Her hair was swept up into a beehive, and she was
wearing a fitted lilac dress. I'd only seen her in dresses
the color of putty or rubber bands or the skin on old lady's
elbows.

"What are you looking at?" she said.

"Nothing. You."

"Nothing. Me. Why, thanks very much."

"Sorry. I mean, you look nice. I like your hair."

She smiled but not in the usual way, not like she was
just throwing you off guard before socking you with a
zinger.

"Thank you." She gave her bangs a tug. "Not too much?"

"No. It's very flattering."

Mrs. Smees had a small waist and slim calves. Without
the scowl, she was actually sort of pretty.

"It's our anniversary. I usually duck out early to get my hair done, but Rita was booked all afternoon. Had to take what I could get. Hope it won't be all wilted by the time Walt gets here for dinner."

"I'm sure it'll be fine." I smiled. She smiled. We got back to work. Two happy lovebirds biding time until we got to see our men. Mrs. Smees actually hummed along to the radio.

She shooed me out at ten after five. I raced back to the cabin with my new jacket and changed. I still had that lipstick Mrs. Welsh had given me. I put it on but couldn't decide. I stared at myself in the mirror and tried to hear what the Seven would have to say. Malou would have liked it. She liked everything. Sara would have said pink was my color. Toni would have said, *You're wearing lipstick to go fishing?*

I wiped it off. Didn't want to look too eager. (Or did I? And what's too eager anyway? These are the things no one tells you.)

I ran through the woods behind the cabin but stopped to catch my breath before crossing into the yard at the Adairs'. I could see Eddie's tin boat docked at the wharf but didn't see him until he grabbed me from behind, and even then I mostly saw just his legs (tanned, hairy) and his sneakers (large, hole in toe of right foot) as he ran up the hill with me under his arm, bleating and helpless as a lost lamb, only a whole lot happier.

"Put that poor girl down, Eddie." A lady rapped at the kitchen window, not quite laughing. "You're not rustling cattle, for goodness' sake."

I stood up, tucked in my shirt, straightened my shorts. Mortified. Eddie dragged me inside, snickering.

The lady was plump and white-haired, a little round hen. She was wearing an apron and tending to various pots on the stove and bowls on the counter. A circle of pastry was rolled out on a sheet of wax paper.

"So you're the famous Dot," she said. "Clara Naylor. I'd shake your hand, but mine are—" She held them up, powdery with flour. "Eddie tells me you could use a decent meal."

Even more mortified. "You made all this for me?"

"Heavens no. I still come in twice a week to cook. Nothing to put a few extra potatoes in the pot." She peered into the oven for a second, then got back to her pastry. "So tell me about yourself, Dot. I'm presuming you're not from these parts, or Eddie would have found you sooner, pretty eyes like that."

Eddie was dipping his finger into a bowl. "She's from Hope. I saw her on the train a couple of weeks ago. Snapped her right up."

"Really?" Mrs. Naylor dusted her hands on her apron, turned and looked at me. "Hope?"

"Just outside."

"Pretty part of the world."

"You've been there?"

"Oh yes. Lived there as a girl. Didn't I hear the orphanage just burned down?"

I must have gone white.

"Oh dear! Didn't mean to upset you. You knew people there?"

"Um. Well—" I was stuttering, trying to cover up. Eddie jumped in.

"Dot was in a fire when she was little."

Mrs. Naylor put her hand on her throat. "Goodness, child. Well, let's not talk about that anymore, shall we? So what brings you here?"

I tried to look brave instead of just relieved. "I heard the resort had jobs. I'm working as a seamstress."

"For Muriel? My. You're holding up well." She smiled at Eddie—a secret joke. "So you two going to eat here, or should I pack it up?"

He was juggling a piece of too-hot piecrust around in his mouth. "Pack it, please. I want to get to the shoals before someone takes my spot."

"Your spot. Only you would think you own a spot of water on the lake." She tucked package after package into a picnic basket. "Coke?"

"Lime Rickey."

"I'll be right back then." She turned the heat down under a couple of pots, then headed out of the room.

Eddie and I sat down. I whispered, "Shouldn't we help her?"

He put his hand on the back of my neck and whispered too. "No. Don't want to act like we think she's old. She wouldn't like that."

"And here I thought you were just being lazy." His hair tickled my lips.

"Me? I told you. I'm nice to old people. I never help them."

And then there was a noise—a little one, the squeak of a shoe on tile or a new breath in the room, something as small as that—and we jumped apart, guilty as sin.

A man was standing in the doorway.

Not *a* man. *The* man. The man I'd spilled coffee on in the restaurant, the man with the crazy face. He'd changed his shirt but not his face.

"Uncle Len!" Eddie was up and over to him, shaking his hand, patting his arm.

The man was staring at me. A tendon jumped in his neck.

"You've met Dot?" Eddie said, like we were at some cocktail party. The man turned away.

"I don't know her."

"Well, here's your chance."

"I said I don't know her!" I thought he was going to hit Eddie.

"Why don't you sit down, Uncle Len?"

"I don't want to sit down." He knocked Eddie's arm away. "There's nothing the matter with me."

Mrs. Naylor bustled back in. "Smelled the pastries, did you, Len?" He turned to her, his face still twitching. "I'll have to pick up some ice cream for you. Best with ice cream, aren't they, Len?"

His chest heaved up and down, but eventually he nodded.

She looked at us. "He loves my turnovers. Here's your Lime Rickey. Now, why don't you two get going?"

"We could stay for a while if you'd like," Eddie said.

"No, no." Then she mouthed, "He'll be fine."

Eddie took the basket, kissed Mrs. Naylor and said, "We going to the drive-in this week, Len?" But the man didn't say anything. He just turned and walked out of the room.

We were anchored at the shoals, our fishing poles baited and in the water, by the time I found the courage to confess. "I have something to tell you."

Eddie put down the reel he was attempting to untangle. "Oh, good. Let me get comfortable." He leaned back against the bow of the boat and twiddled his toes against my shin.

I told him the whole story about Mr. Peters and me—at least, the whole story minus the part he would have liked the best: the fact that I was only in the dining room to sneak a look at him.

"That's it?" As in *so what?*

"I didn't know he was your uncle."

"You mean you only scald people I'm not related to?"

"I mean, it just makes it worse knowing he's your uncle."

"I have a confession too." He took my hand and looked deep into my eyes. "He's not my uncle. So go ahead. Scald away! He's all yours."

I laughed. Maybe this wasn't that big a deal after all. "Why do you call him uncle then?"

"He grew up with Dad. The three of them. Dad, Len and Ward Adair. Buckminster boys."

"So what's his story? Was he always like that?"

"No, but for as long as I've known him. Len used to be quiet, sort of an egghead, Dad says. Then the war came. He ended up as a medic in Italy. I guess it was a bloodbath. He was pretty messed up when he came back and only got worse. His girlfriend left him. His parents couldn't handle him. The Adairs have the extra cabin, so they took him in. Ward's looked after him ever since."

"Nice thing to do."

"I don't think Ward would say that. He and Dad both feel pretty guilty about Len. The poor guy didn't want to go to war. He was a pacifist. Wanted to be a science teacher. He'd already done a couple of years at the university, but they badgered him into it. Ward and Dad were the hotshots around here back then. Everyone looked up to them. They made him out to be a sissy, so he signed up. They both got wounded early on, came back heroes. Len suffered through all six years, came back a basket case." Eddie shrugged, sad, maybe a little ashamed.

I wanted to say the right thing, but before I could even think of what that might be, he said, "Hungry?" Smiling again.

I was.

There were meat pies and potato salad and chicken sandwiches. Flakes of pastry freckled Eddie's lips and then the back of his arm when he wiped them away.

I dug into the potato salad. It was creamy and salty and a little tangy from the chunks of pickle.

"Good?" he asked.

"I'm in heaven," I said.

Sixteen

I HAD TROUBLE sleeping again that night, and it wasn't just from thinking about Eddie. I'd drift off for a while, then there'd be a little noise—a twig snapping or a branch brushing against the window—and I'd lurch up, sure I was in the fire again or that someone was trying to break into the cabin.

I'd sit there paralyzed, my knees against my chest and my heart pounding, until I managed to convince myself that it was just the wind, or an animal, and then I'd unfold myself and try to go to sleep again.

At six thirty, I gave up and went to get some breakfast.

I was locking the cabin door when I noticed it. A bird's wing on my front step. A robin, maybe, or a swallow. Something small-boned like that.

So that's what I heard, I thought. An animal of some sort, leaving me a little gift. I tried to figure out which animals would do that, but nothing came to mind. The wing was so delicate—bleached white, stripped clean, almost pretty.

Maybe Eddie would know. I took it inside and put it on my bedside table. While I was there, I decided to grab the jacket he'd given me. It was cool that early in the day.

I headed over to the staff cafeteria. Glennie was just leaving. She had a mug in her hand and bags under her eyes. Her skin was the color of uncooked pastry.

"You okay?"

"Bad case of ginfluenza. Just heading to bed now. But not to worry, darling." Brave smile. "Plenty of rest and the latest issue of *Glamour*, and I should be all better by cocktail hour. Hey…"

She reached out and rubbed the sleeve of my jacket. "Eddie give you this?"

"Yeah. How'd you know?"

"I recognize it." She pulled back my collar and checked the label. She smelled of Nivea cream and something sour. "Yup. Holt's Junior Miss. That's Libby's."

"Libby?" I didn't understand.

"Eddie's conquest of 1963."

I couldn't get the jacket off fast enough.

"No. Stop. Enjoy it. She's not here this year—and anyway, that girl has more clothes than she knows what to do with. I'm sure that's not the only garment she left at his place." Glennie dipped her fingers into her hot tea, pulled out the bag and tossed it on the ground. "Oh, and speaking of delectable young men…a bunch of us are going into town Saturday night for some fries. Interested in coming along?"

"Don't think I can." *I'll be in my cabin sobbing.*

"Sure? Finlay will be there..."

I shook my head. Another good reason not to go.

"Neither French fries nor Finlay can lure you out? I admire your self-restraint. Offer me a couple of stale Cheezies and anyone younger than Oliphant, and I'd be there like a shot." She laughed at herself, then headed into the Harem.

I'd lost my appetite. I took a table near the back of the cafeteria and sat there, picking at my toast, hating my jacket, hating Libby and Glennie and maybe Eddie too.

I found this at the cottage and thought it would look good on you. That's all he'd said in his note. Not as if he claimed to have bought it for me or anything. I wasn't at the Arms last year. Why shouldn't Eddie have had a girlfriend back then? Who cares about Libby?

That's what I told myself. But the walls of the cafeteria were covered with old staff photos, and I couldn't resist checking out the 1963 group shot.

Libby Braithewaite wasn't hard to find. She was slim and blond and utterly, tragically pretty.

⁓

Mrs. Smees didn't look up when I came in to work.

"How was your anniversary?" I said.

She slapped down her pencil. Her beehive drooped to one side like a tent missing a pole. "My personal life any business of yours?"

All I needed. The jacket. Libby's face. And now Mrs. Smees in one of her moods.

The morning dragged on. The *EddieEddieEddie* of the sewing machine just reminded me of all the other girls cooing his name and how much prettier than me they were.

Eddie stuck his head in the door at five after four. That smile. He probably didn't even remember whose jacket it was. "My two favorite gals! Isn't it time you called it a day?"

"Take her, if you want. I got work to do." Mrs. Smees squared a pile of papers on her desk and slammed the stapler through it with the heel of her hand.

Eddie looked at me like, *What's up with her?* I gave him a tight little shake of my head. A warning. He laughed at my fear and launched himself onto the edge of her desk.

"Oh hey, Muriel. I'm doing a story I thought you might be able to help me with."

"Didn't I just say I have work to do?"

"You can staple and talk at the same time. I know you can. Seen you do it—"

She slapped down another ream of paper and looked at him with that mean little smile. "Okay. What?"

Didn't bother him at all. "You were at the Arms in '47, weren't you?"

"No. I was at the Adairs' then."

"Close enough. Must have been very young."

"Get on with it, Eddie."

"I'm writing an article on the Bye-Bye Baby. What really happened that night."

"Oh for the love of God." She grabbed a bunch of files and got up from her desk, her chair spinning out behind her. "That's what you're wasting my time with? Load of nonsense, the whole thing."

"You mean the disappearing baby? I know that didn't happen."

"So what are you writing about then?" She yanked open the filing cabinet and started shoving papers in.

"The truth. People saw a real baby there that night. Where did it come from? Who was the—"

Mrs. Smees whammed the cabinet shut so hard my fillings rang. "Is news that slow, Eddie, that you have to report on some hogwash a bunch of drunken teenagers made up decades ago?"

"That's the thing. I don't think they made it up."

"You don't? Well, I do. And I should know. I was there."

Eddie reared back, a laugh stuttering in his throat.

"What's so funny?"

"You were at the clearing that night?"

She started counting the pillowcases for the third time that day.

"Yes, I was. You're not the first person to be young, you know. And I'm telling you, there was no baby, disappearing or not. There was just a bunch of snotty-nosed college kids with more money than brains thinking it would be funny to stir things up for a while. I'm sure you know the type. So do yourself a favor. Drop the whole thing. Now, why don't the two of you get out of here and let me get my damn work done."

Seventeen

IT WAS ALL part of our investigation. That's what Eddie claimed, and it seemed like a good excuse. We waited until dark and then headed up to the clearing.

"See what I mean?" he said as we fumbled through the woods, the flashlight giving off a dim yellow cone of light. "You'd never find the way if you didn't know where it was. That's why I think it had to be someone from around here."

A tree blocked the path. "Under or over?" he said, then scooped me up and over it.

"You can put me down now."

"I could." He didn't. "I feel like I should be hunchbacked and cackling madly as I whisk the terrified maiden off to my forest lair."

"Your cackle wouldn't terrify me."

"You haven't heard my cackle."

"Well, if it's anything like your chortle, it wouldn't scare me at all."

"Know what I don't understand?"

"What?" Another joke.

"No. I'm being serious. If the mother was from around here, why would she go to the clearing to have her baby? She'd know there could be kids up here."

At the moment, it was difficult caring a whole lot about trivial matters like what my mother was thinking the night she had me, but I did my best to focus.

"Didn't Sandra say no one ever came up on Tuesdays? If the mother'd known that, she probably figured it was safe. Maybe she didn't know the dance was canceled."

"You're an excellent addition to our investigative team, Miss Blythe."

He trudged on through the woods, me in his arms, not saying much. I kept thinking I might actually have a boyfriend. I imagined lying in bed in the dark at the Home, telling Sara or Tess all about him.

Then I realized Tess probably wouldn't have been there. She'd have snuck out through the window to see her own boyfriend. And the idea just popped into my head.

"She was meeting someone," I said. "Didn't you say that tree's sort of a landmark?"

He laughed the way you do when something's right. "Think they were going to run away together?"

"I don't even know who *they* are. I feel like we're just making this story up."

"Fun, isn't it?" He put me down. "*Et voilà!* The clearing."

The moon was high and bright and turned everything shades of blue. The clearing wasn't much bigger than Mrs. Smees's office. The forest floor had been worn down to bare earth except in the middle, where there was a dark circle of rocks and the ashy remains of a fire. I heard a truck honk in the distance, but otherwise the only sounds were the scuffles of our feet and the rustle of leaves.

"Got your bearings?" Eddie said.

"Not really."

He pointed with the flashlight. "The highway, north. We're pretty close, actually. The Arms, south. Then all the way down the west side, over there, the road into the resort."

"And beyond the road are the guest cottages, right? And then what? The Adairs' place?"

"Yup."

"What about over there?"

"To the east? Woods, woods, woods and then Miss Cameron's. You'd have to be Alexander the Great to figure out how to get in from that side."

"Maybe the mother came in during the day. While it was light."

"She'd still need a machete."

"Sounds like one of those magazines Bas reads while he's waiting for the wash. Machete Mama."

"Machete Mama and the Disappearing Baby."

"I'd read it."

"Who wouldn't?" He waved the flashlight around the clearing. "Okay. Let's see if we can figure this out. We know there were about twenty kids here. Mostly drunk. Our informant, the former Sandra Smithers, is huddled by the fire when she notices a townie named Dougie Pratt romancing a college girl named Cecily Ingram. A re-creation of events might help, don't you think?"

"Sure. I'll play Cecily—or do you want to?"

"No. Please. Ladies first." He took my hand and led me to the far side of the fire circle. "So I imagine they'd be around here. Dougie's been eying Cecily all night. He's moved by the glow the fire casts on her chestnut hair, the way the flames dance in her opalescent eyes, etcetera, etcetera. Maybe someone brought a guitar and is playing, um—what's a hit song from around 1947?"

"'Boogie Woogie Bugle Boy'?"

"Very romantic. But okay. Doug takes another swig of rum—"

"Gin. Sandra says it was gin."

"—gin, then screws up his courage and asks her to dance. Miss Ingram? May I?"

I shrug like, *Why not?*

"Much to Dougie's astonishment, she says yes."

Eddie put one arm around my back and took my hand with the other. "They glide expertly around the clearing… you call that gliding?"

"Sorry. Not much of a dancer. You knew that going into this."

"She isn't much of a dancer, and yet there's something magnetic about Cecily Ingram. She pulls him closer—are you listening?"

"I'm concentrating on gliding."

He wrapped my arm around his neck. "Cecily pulls him closer and whispers in his ear…"

"This is getting silly."

"No, that's not what she says. She says, 'Take me to the tree, my darling.' He doesn't need to be told twice. He spins her through one last pirouette, then discreetly leads her out of the clearing."

Eddie found another path, and we sort of danced along that for a minute or two, until we came to a large boulder.

"Careful," he said. "This is where I chipped my tooth." I did my best not to think how that happened. He tiptoed me around the backside of the rock. "And here we are. The tree!"

"The tree," I said.

"So this is where Dougie and Cecily would have come."

"Uh-huh. Yeah."

And suddenly we were awkward, two strangers stuck making conversation at a bus stop.

I said, "Guess it hasn't changed much since then."

"Little bigger maybe." He put his hands in his pockets, shrugged.

"Oh, right. They grow, don't they?"

"Trees? So I've heard."

"But not boulders."

"No."

We'd come all this way. All the joking and the whispering and the almost-accidental touching and not-so-accidental touching and then to just stand here like this, talking nonsense. I thought of Joe and that screen door creaking between scared and excited.

"They probably weren't standing," I said.

"No. Unlikely."

"Well, maybe we shouldn't."

"Not if we're re-creating it, I guess."

I took his hand, and we sat on the ground.

"You think they'd be sitting?" I said.

"Doubt it."

I lay down. He lay down beside me. Two corpses in the morgue. I could see the Big Dipper and the North Star. I was pretty sure Doug and Cecily hadn't been looking at constellations either.

I cleared my throat. Eddie rolled over onto his side, facing me.

"I was thinking about it, and my guess is he probably had his arm around her," he said. "Like this maybe."

I said, "I don't want to play this game anymore."

"Oh," Eddie said and moved away.

I pulled him back. "Why don't we kiss for real?"

Eighteen

I NEVER WANTED to leave. I'd have been happy spending the rest of my life in the woods, cut off from civilization, surviving on nothing more than a diet of ferns and berries and Eddie. But we apparently had lives to get back to.

He helped me to my feet. I was cold when I stepped away from him, so he opened his shirt and wrapped me in it. It was hard going in the woods in the dark, even with his arm around me, and, oddly, that made me think of my mother.

"How'd she do it?"

"Hmm?" Eddie seemed a bit dozy. Neither of us had gotten quite enough oxygen in the last little while.

"The mother. How'd she make it out of the woods? She must have been exhausted after the birth, and it's a long way."

"She might have gone the other way." He didn't sound that interested.

"There's another way?"

"An old logging road. Pretty much grown over. It's shorter, but it takes you out to the resort road, not down through the woods. Not many people know about it."

"Show me."

Big whimper. "We'd have to go back to the clearing again."

"It's your article." He laughed and muttered something in my ear that I didn't quite hear but liked the sound of.

We backtracked to the tree, skirted around the heart-shaped rock and found the logging road. The ground was higher here, and when Eddie pointed the flashlight I could just make out the clearing below. We walked for a while, and then he suddenly stopped.

"One more thing you should see, since you dragged me all this way…" He waved his flashlight over a large squarish hole in the forest floor, three feet deep or so, just off to the side of the path. "The famous Passion Pit."

I peered into it. "It almost looks man-made."

"Dad said there used to be a hunting cabin back here when he was a kid. I'm guessing this is all that's left of it." Then he whispered into my hair, "We should check it out sometime."

I was past the point of blushing.

We headed out onto the logging road. In no time, we were scrabbling through bushes and onto the long driveway into the resort. I recognized where we were. Couldn't have been any more than a few minutes to the highway.

"We made it," I said.

"Yes, we did." Hands in my hair. "I think we should celebrate." Legs on either side of mine. Lips on my neck.

And then a car rounded the corner, lighting us up like prisoners caught scaling the jailhouse wall. I jumped away, my arm across my face.

The car stopped. The window rolled down, a man stuck out his head.

"Eddie."

"Uncle Ward." It was the man I'd seen with Mr. Peters in the restaurant.

This was Ward Adair.

Eddie pulled me over to the car, leaned his arm against the roof, didn't even try to do anything with his hair, his shirt. "What are you doing out at this hour?"

"I could ask you the same thing." Mr. Adair was unshaven and bleary-eyed but when he smiled, handsome as a spy. "But I won't."

Eddie laughed. "This is Dot."

"How do you do? Mrs. Naylor said I'd probably meet you sometime soon. Didn't imagine it would be at three in the morning."

I went red, a hot spot in the darkness.

"Three?" Eddie laughed. "Why *are* you out?"

"Looking for Len. Haven't seen him, have you?"

"Not another one of his bad spells?"

"Yeah. Last couple of weeks. He's back to his wandering again. Usually shows up by morning, but Clara's all in a knot about it."

"Can I help?"

Mr. Adair shook his head. "You take your girl back before you get her in more trouble than you already have. I'll find him. I know his ways better than anyone. Two old bachelors. We're worse than a married couple."

He raised two fingers in a wave, then headed off toward the highway.

Eddie and I snuck back into the colony. He kissed me goodbye on the stairs to my cabin. It was dark, so I didn't notice the bones on the step until the next day.

Nineteen

IT WAS ANOTHER bird's wing. White and fragile. A piece of art.

If I hadn't been so tired—and so happy—when I found it the next morning, I might have been concerned. My imagination might have come up with some gruesome explanation for why, yet again, there were bones on my front step. Luckily, my imagination was otherwise occupied. I hid the wing under the stairs and raced off to work. I'd tell Eddie about it later.

I was going to be working all weekend. The annual Dunbrae Garden Party was on Sunday, so everyone had been called in, but I was meeting him that night at the newspaper office to go through old issues of the *Gleaner*. He wanted to double-ride me in after work, but I told him I'd meet him there because I had something to do for Mrs. Smees.

That was a lie. It was Friday. The night the ladies' auxiliary of St. Ninian's Anglican Church got together. I took the bus into Buckminster after dinner.

I pushed open the front door to the church and walked in. No one was there. I was starting to wonder if the nurse had given me the wrong night when I heard someone say, "May I help you?"

A lady came out from behind the big bouquet of flowers on the altar.

"Mrs. Naylor?" We were both surprised to see each other.

"Dot. Just getting ready for the baptism tomorrow. What are you doing here?"

"Looking for the ladies' auxiliary."

"You're a little young for that, but you're more than welcome to join us. We're meeting in the church hall in ten minutes."

"No. I'm not joining. I just need some help."

"Oh dear." She bustled toward me, worried.

"It's nothing. I'd just like to know who this belongs to. Someone said you ladies might recognize the crest."

I handed her the spoon.

"What's this?" She looked at me with the weirdest expression on her face.

"I think it's a mustard spoon."

"Oh. Yes. Of course." She shook her head like, *Silly me.* "Tiny, isn't it?"

"Don't suppose you'd know whose family motto that is."

She put on her glasses and studied it for quite a while. "Hmm. That's a new one to me. 'Loyal unto death.'"

"That's what it says? I thought it said *loyal on the earth.*"

She took another look. "Oh, yes. You're right! Loyal on the earth. That still doesn't help me, but I'm sure one of my friends will recognize it. We've got some avid genealogists. Mind if I keep it?"

"No. Please."

She put it into her apron pocket, then turned to go. "Sorry, dear. Have to run. The ladies are very particular about getting our meetings started on time."

They really must have been, given how fast she beetled out of there.

 *

The sign outside the newspaper office said *The Buckminster Gleaner. News, Views and all the Who's Who of Cottage Country.* Eddie pulled me behind it for a kiss. We were just stepping back out when the editor walked out the door, swabbing his neck with a hankie the size of a small tablecloth.

"How's your piece on the new highway coming, Ed?"

"Almost done. Have it on your desk by tomorrow night, if that's okay."

"Should be." Mr. Quigley patted Eddie's shoulder, put on his hat and tipped his head to me. "Gotta fly. I'm meeting Ward and Len at the golf course in ten minutes."

"So he found him then?" Eddie said. "We saw Ward out looking last night."

"Yeah. Len was wandering around out behind the resort, scaring the guests again." Mr. Quigley shook his head.

"Could you give Ward a break and get Len out fishing? He'll go with you."

"Already picked us up some nice trout flies. Thought I'd take Dad out too."

"Good man. Gunky must be the only one who can get a smile out of Len these days."

"You know Dad. Won't give up until he does."

⟳

The newspaper office was empty, but you could still smell the sticky residue of cigarettes and the men who smoked them. Eddie's desk was squeezed into a corner at the back, a two-foot pile of newspapers stacked on top of it.

He picked up the first one. "Tuesday, July 8, 1947. Day of the party. I figured there wouldn't be any reason to start before then. All things considered, I doubt anybody had a baby shower for the mother."

We looked through two weeks of the *Gleaner* without much luck. The prime minister was arriving in town on the ninth for his niece's engagement party and the whole town was in a flurry over that. Lots of birth announcements too, but they were all of the usual "Mr. and Mrs. Donald B. Jackson are delighted…" variety. None of the "A premature baby was discovered…" type. There were no reports of a woman being admitted to the hospital or found bleeding and disoriented in the woods. Nothing about a wild party or a corpse either.

We did, however, see lots of ribbon cuttings, grumpy church ladies and little kids beaming their faces off over first-place prizes in three-legged races and tap-dancing competitions. In the regular "Dunbrae Doings" section, there was a photo of women in long gowns and bare shoulders, laughing over cocktails at a party celebrating the Adair Scholarship Fund.

"Adair?" I said. "Like Ward Adair?"

"Yup. Every year his family sends 'a deserving young Buckminsterite' to university."

"Such as yourself?"

"Nah. I'd kind of like to make my own way. Ward's done enough for the Nicholsons as it is." He shrugged, then changed the subject by pointing out everyone in the picture. Only two names rang a bell. Miss Augusta Cameron, looking even more like Cleopatra because her hair was dark back then. And Helena Rathburn. It was obvious from whom Glennie had inherited her smile—and her bosom.

Not much going on at the resort the following week, at least according to the *Gleaner*. We were squinting at a photo of the then-new staff cafeteria, trying to figure out if the pretty woman at the side could possibly have been Ida forty pounds ago, when a door opened behind us and a big guy with a fresh crewcut lumbered in.

Eddie introduced us. Jimmy Sweeny had little eyes and a nose like an old boot but a nice smile. (He flashed it at me when Eddie tried to pass me off as his assistant.) He swung a chair around and sat on it backward, beefy arms crossed on the top rail.

"Those the issues you looking for?"

"Yeah, thanks, Jim. Hope it wasn't too much trouble tracking them down for me."

"No trouble at all. It's my job. What'd you want them for anyway?"

"Doing a story on Bye-Bye Baby."

"The party up Dunbrae?"

"No. The real thing. I heard someone saw an actual baby that night."

"Huh." Jimmy turned down his lips and nodded. The classic well-whaddya-know face, but he didn't manage to pull it off very well.

Eddie noticed that too. "What do you mean, *huh*?"

"Just huh." He hooked a finger behind the knot in his tie and wiggled it down an inch or two. "Awful hot in here, eh?"

"Were you there?" Eddie was suddenly alert, a wolf on a scent.

"No."

"Jimmy."

"What?"

"You were there, weren't you?"

"No. I wasn't." He scratched the side of his face. His whiskers made a sound like a fingernail being filed. "At least, not *there* there."

"Speak English, Jim."

There was a long pause. Jimmy skidded his hands down his thighs, looked around the newsroom.

"You know something." Eddie wasn't going to let it go.

"Not really. I got no proof. And even if I did, you'd only think I was telling you because her and Joanie don't get along no more."

"No, I wouldn't. Tell me what?"

Jimmy put his fists on his knees, let some air out. "Off the record?"

"Yes. Scout's honor."

"And Dot here?"

"She's not going to say anything either."

I crossed my heart.

Another long pause, then: "I'm only telling you this, Eddie, because I don't want you stepping on the wrong toes. Might even help you know when to shut up—although that strikes me as unlikely."

We laughed dutifully, and then Jimmy took a big breath, as if he was going to blow up a balloon, and began to talk.

"So this was when me and Joanie was dating. I was working here, but as soon as the supper bell rang, I'd hop in my '39 Ford and burn up Highway 7 to see her. Wouldn't make it home before two, but I'd be at work first thing the next morning, bright as a new penny. Young love, eh? Anyway, I was driving home that night. Just made the turn past Kendall's Landing and there's this car off the road. Came up on me pretty fast. Had to slam on the brakes, and even so I almost hit her. Dark hair, dark dress, changing the tire. Barely saw her."

"Saw who?"

"Muriel. Didn't I say that already?"

"Muriel Smees?" Eddie and I said it at the same time.

Jimmy smiled. "That's good luck, you know. Saying things together. Me and Joanie always go *jinx* and—"

Eddie was sitting up straight in his chair, elbows flat on the armrests, like someone had just hit him with a jolt of electricity. "You saw Muriel Smees on the side of the road the night the baby was born." Neither of us had really believed it when she said she'd been at the clearing.

Jimmy gave a slow nod. "I know. Surprised me too. Didn't think Muriel knew how to drive. Never seen her drive, before or since. Can't imagine she'd know how to change a tire."

"Whose car?" I asked.

"Didn't recognize it. Black one. Not theirs. Walt didn't get a car until '52, '53, something like that."

Eddie nodded.

"So I says, *Got a problem, Muriel?* And she pops up with the tire iron in her hand like she's going to haul off and lambaste me. You're probably not surprised—but Muriel wasn't that way back then. Never was a barrel of fun, but, believe it or not, she wasn't always mad at the world. I went, *Muriel, it's me, Jimmy*, and she went, *Oh, didn't recognize you.*"

He snorted. "Not recognize me? I'm four inches and fifty pounds bigger than any man in these parts, and I've known her all my life. But I let it go. People are strange. I says, *Let me do that for you.* I go to take the tire iron from her and she says, *No, Jimmy, I don't need your help.*"

He pulled back his chin and looked first at Eddie, then at me.

"*I don't need help from the likes of you.* That's the way she says it. Now, she'd moved up in the world and was working for the Adairs back then, but that don't make any difference. We're both just townies. One's no better than the other. I had half a mind to get in my truck and go. But ditch a woman on the side of the road? Not my style. I says, *Then I'll drive you home and come back for the car tomorrow.* Well. You should have seen the look on her face. As if I was going to get her alone and do something unspeakable to her. I'm not that type of guy."

"No. You're not, Jimmy." I got the feeling Eddie just wanted to move the story along.

"So we have this standoff, her up against the car, refusing to budge, me with my hands on my hips, neither of us willing to give an inch. Then all of a sudden she flicks her chin up and says, *You go get Walt. I'll stay here until he comes for me. I'll be fine.*

"No convincing her otherwise. So I says okay and reach out to put my hand on her shoulder, just to reassure her like, and she flinches. You know, kind of moves her head to the side. That's when I see someone lying in the backseat. And I know Muriel saw me see it too. *You better get going,* she says, sweet as pie, as if she's worried I'll be late for tea. I should have asked what was up then, but I didn't. She was working too hard to distract me, so what was the point? I told her to get in the car and lock the door, and then I drove into town and woke up Walt."

"Know who was in the backseat?" Eddie was practically panting.

"No. I just saw legs. A lady's legs. I figured one of her girlfriends got herself drunk and Muriel was trying to sneak her home without anyone seeing. Never would have thought any different, but then rumors started circulating about that disappearing baby, and I found myself getting suspicious. Truth is, I couldn't imagine a single one of Muriel's friends passed-out drunk. Those girls wouldn't take a nip on New Year's Eve if the pope himself were pouring."

He had a little chuckle at that.

"But by the same token, her friends weren't the type to give birth in the woods neither. So maybe I'm way off base here. See why I wouldn't want this published? All speculation. Never even told Joanie. Lady in the back might justa got a bad perm she couldn't bear anyone seeing. Joanie didn't step outside for a month after her sister gave her one. Might be a perfectly innocent explanation for the whole thing. I've just never had the courage to ask Muriel what that might be. And now, with her and Joanie at each other's throats over that IODE dinner, guess I never will."

"Any chance Mrs. Smees was the mother?" I asked, sick at the thought.

"Nah. If Muriel were the mother, wouldn't she be the one in the backseat? Even she ain't tough enough to be changing a tire right after pushing a baby out."

He sighed and scratched his big head. "I feel awful bad about that night."

"Why?" Eddie said. "You didn't do anything wrong."

"Not sure about that. Muriel was in a bad way. I could see that. I should have stood my ground. I brought Walt back but can't imagine he was much good to her, given how he was after the war. No better than a robot. That's what I tell Joanie when she gets on a rant about her. Say what you will about Muriel Smees, but she's not a bad person. Walt come back a different man than the one she married, but she stuck by him. More than you can say for a lot of girls around here."

There was an awkward silence. Then Jimmy banged his hand against his chair and popped up.

"Oh Lord. Sorry, Eddie. Wasn't talking about Dorcas. Salt of the earth, your mother. No one would blame her. I was talking about someone else. Honestly. Thinking of someone else entirely."

Eddie waved it off. "I know you weren't, Jimmy. We all know what Dad's like."

"Not saying anything about Gunky neither. Love the guy. Like a big brother to me."

Jimmy's head lolled back and forth as if he had lead weights hanging from his ears. "I sure managed to do more than my fair share of damage for one day. Joanie's right. I should save my big mouth for eating. What goes in causes a lot less trouble than what comes out."

Twenty

I WANTED TO find my parents. I wanted to find out who I was, where I came from, all that stuff. But that was only part of it now and not even the best part.

I was in it now mostly for other reasons. The way Eddie's face kind of lit up when I mentioned something he hadn't thought of yet. The way we didn't even have to look at each other to know we were both thinking the same thing. The way we could sit happily for hours, ruminating on the craziest scenarios. It was like the best daydream I'd ever had. A wild story racing ahead of me. My imagination, for once, the little fat kid at the back, screaming, "Wait for me! Wait for me!"

We stayed up late that night on the steps of the seamstress's cabin, chewing on the idea of Mrs. Smees being mixed up in this whole business.

The mother?

Jimmy seemed positive it wasn't her baby.

The accomplice?

More likely, although that was strange too. We both knew Mrs. Smees didn't have her driver's license. She hitched a ride into work every morning with Mr. Oliphant, and every morning she said the same thing: *Worth learning to drive if only so I never have to put up with that yakking of his again.*

"Maybe that whole experience turned her off driving?" I said.

"What whole experience?"

"Finding the mother bleeding on the side of the road, having to get her to safety, spirit the baby out of town..."

"That's what happened?"

"Well. Um. Maybe. I don't know. Do you?"

"No," he said. "I don't know anything."

And maybe we were just tired, but somehow that struck us as funny, not knowing anything, and we began lobbing out other ideas for how a girl could have found herself curled up in the back of a car driven by Mrs. Smees, and maybe we started with more or less plausible suggestions, I can't remember, but things wobbled out of hand pretty fast, and soon we were gasping out truly appalling ideas about kidnapped babies and dead seamstresses, tears streaming down our faces, lips right against each other's ears, bodies slack from laughing and—what seemed to me, at least— utter joy. I was never so thankful to have been an abandoned baby in my entire life.

It must have been two or three in the morning before Eddie tiptoed out of the colony, shoes in one hand, hair like a startled cat's, and even then I couldn't bear for him to go.

Twenty-One

AT LUNCHTIME THE next day, I grabbed a sandwich from the cafeteria, then ran back through the rain to buy a postcard at the lodge's front desk. I was going to write Mrs. Hazelton, tell her all about my new life. (Except the Eddie part. I wanted her to be proud of me, not hopping the next train and dragging me back to Hope by the ear he'd just been nibbling on.)

I was trying to decide between three postcards when I heard a little girl shouting, "Spot! Spo-ot!" I figured she'd just lost her dog so didn't turn around until I felt someone yanking at my sleeve.

"Spot! How come you didn't answer me?" And there was Jody looking up at me, the wobbly red face of a dictator over the grubby yellow bathing suit of a six-year-old.

"Because it's Dot, sweetie," Sandra said, staggering into view, little Wendy in one hand, a cigarette in the other. "Dot with a *D*—like *demon* or *despair*. Now, here's a nickel.

Take your sister down to the canteen and buy yourself some junk. I'll be there in a sec."

She was smiling like a perfect mother as she watched them go, but she muttered, "Thinks she rules the world, that one. Sorry about that."

"No. She's cute."

"For about ten minutes. Try taking a full day of it. I'm going to lose my mind if it doesn't stop raining. I put them in swimming lessons specifically so I could get an hour of peace a day. And then they cancel the lessons? Kids can't swim in the rain?"

She let out a low growl. The man at the front desk smiled apologetically. I decided to buy all three postcards.

"Oh, listen," Sandra said. "Seeing Eddie anytime soon?"

"Tonight."

"Could you tell him something for me?"

"Sure."

She waved me over to the far side of the lobby, away from a bridge game that had just gotten started near the fireplace.

"I remembered something about that party." She whispered like a Bond girl passing on government secrets. "Eddie's mentioning the pit was what did it. There was a girl named Lois—Kincaid, I think—who claimed to have seen something. There were all sorts of wild stories floating around back then, but Lois seemed really serious. Said she saw somebody that night, a man, sneaking through the woods. He had something in his arms, and she was pretty sure it was a baby."

Eddie was going to love this. That was the first thing I thought.

"Did she tell anybody about it?"

"Other than us? Ooh, I doubt it. Nobody wanted to draw any attention to what went on in the clearing. The booze, the necking, etcetera—and now a baby? The grown-ups would have shut it down for good. Crokinole in the staff cafeteria and lights-out at ten for the rest of the summer. Didn't want that."

"Is Lois still around?"

"Haven't seen her for years. That's why I wasn't going to mention it—but then this morning I remembered who she was dating. She was in the pit that night with the Simmonds boy."

"And he's around?"

"Yes. I think Bas works in the laundry here or something."

"Bas? Bas was there?"

"I'm sure of it. He was at all the parties. Bad boy—but very popular. And not just because he was such a looker. He had some kind of in with the bootlegger. A cousin maybe? We always figured he'd end up in jail—had a bit of an issue with authority, as I recall—but he managed to keep his nose clean. I bet he'd know something."

Almost too good to be true. "Mrs. Smees was there that night too, wasn't she?"

"Muriel? At the clearing? You're joking, right?"

"No. That's what I heard."

"Well, you heard wrong. If Muriel had been there, no one else would have been. Absolute killjoy, that girl—and anyway she was a good five years older than us. She'd never have rolled with that crowd, even if she'd been the type to actually enjoy life occasionally. Muriel…" Sandra sputtered at the utter craziness of the idea, then checked her watch. "Better go. Got to find those girls before they get me barred from the Arms." She sighed. "Again."

Twenty-Two

I WAS BUSTING to talk to Eddie but knew he'd be out of touch all afternoon, repairing the screen at the Adairs' and then getting that article on the new highway done by seven for Monday's paper.

At around three thirty, Mrs. Smees collected an armload of files and headed for the door. "I'll be about fifteen minutes, which isn't an invitation for you to do nothing until I get back."

I made myself sit still until I heard her heels click up the stairs, and then I bundled together a few things that conceivably needed washing and slipped into the laundry room. Bas was at the sink, sleeves bunched up around his elbows, scrubbing at a white tablecloth, a dark-blond hank of hair bouncing over his forehead.

"Peach stains. Bane of my existence." He glanced over his shoulder, then got back at it. "What you got there? Slipcovers? You sure she wants those done?"

"Yeah. Pretty sure. "

He gave his hands a hard snap over the sink, then turned to look at me.

I tried to act normal, but I had the feeling I looked less like I was smiling and more like I'd just asked him if there was spinach between my teeth.

"This isn't about slipcovers, is it?"

"Um. Not exactly. They looked a little dingy, but there's also something I—"

He laughed in his throat and brushed that hair off his forehead. I could sort of see why Sandra thought he was good-looking.

"Could have sworn we'd been through this already. Don't be sneaking around making a fool of me, Dot. Ask your questions. I'll decide whether I want to answer."

"You knew Lois Kincaid?"

"You're worse than my ex-wife. Jealous, are you?"

I gave a polite chuckle.

"Yeah. I knew her. Knew her pretty good for a while. Nice girl, Lois. Great legs."

"Were you with her the night the baby disappeared?"

He stopped smiling. Sandra was right. He'd been there.

"And don't say, 'What baby?'" I said.

"Is that what this is about?" He took a piece of Juicy Fruit out of his pocket, peeled off the wrapper and tucked the gum between his back teeth. He didn't offer me one.

"You saw something, didn't you?"

He turned back to the sink, went after that stain again. I hustled over and stood right beside him.

"A man?"

He didn't answer. I was so excited, so determined to find out. I could just see Eddie's face when I laid it all out for him, wagging my tail like a retriever with a limp duck between my jaws.

Bas dropped the tablecloth, leaned his hands on the edge of the sink, and stared into the water.

"This may come as a surprise to you, Dot, but I got into my share of trouble when I was your age. I'd hate to see that happen to you. You're not poking your nose someplace it shouldn't be?"

I must have paused too long.

"Forget it. Less I know the better, frankly. I got to work late tonight as it is, so scram, if you don't mind. I'm busy."

"This is really important to me, Bas."

He tapped his fingers on the tin sink. Didn't answer.

"You were in the pit with Lois that night, and you saw a man carrying something. I'm right, aren't I?"

He laughed at that, although it wasn't a happy laugh. "What do you know about the pit? Little girl like you."

"Enough."

"Enough to know how dark it is out there?"

"It wasn't dark that night. If you were in the pit, you could have seen someone walking out along that old logging road."

Bas turned, clasped his hands at his waist, took a moment to compose himself.

"Where you from, Dot?"

"Hope." *Or here. Maybe I'm from here. You tell me.*

He curled up his lips and nodded. "Well, you're forgiven then. Can't be expected to know how things work in this neck of the woods, though my guess is Hope ain't a heck of a lot better than Buckminster. Small towns are all the same— and once the summer folk leave, that's all Buckminster is. Another small town with its share of peculiarities and oddballs and things most of us would prefer to forget."

"Such as?"

He gave a little laugh. "When did you get so bold all of a sudden?"

"C'mon, Bas. Such as?"

"I've kept my mouth shut for a long time, and it hasn't hurt me. I will tell you one thing, though, for your own benefit: there are people around here you don't speak ill of, regardless of what you may know about them. Don't give me that look."

"What look?"

"That look. Like you'd have done different. You think you'd have just tromped over to the police station, all righteous indignation, told your story and that would have been that?"

He put on a fake voice. High. Girly. "Sure, it was dark, Officer, but I know it was him. I seen him limping off through the woods, and he was carrying a baby...Well, yes, I did only see him from behind and no, I didn't actually see the child, but it sure as shooting sounded like a baby to me, or maybe a kitten…And, all right, I did have the tiniest bit to drink, Officer…well, maybe slightly more than that, but I know what I saw and, believe me, it was him!"

He stuck out his chin. "How you think that would go over? The word of a couple of soused teenagers against a man everyone—"

He caught himself.

"Everyone what?"

"Doesn't matter. What we saw—or didn't see—don't matter a bit. You think the police were going to bring the wrongdoer to justice just because that's what's supposed to happen in this good world? Well, Dot, I got news for you. Here's what I've learned after almost twenty years of scrubbing the stains out of other people's unmentionables. A lot of folks around here got a lot of secrets hidden behind their money or their charm or the medals pinned to their chest. We opened our mouths about what we saw and nothing good would have come of it. For either of us. And a hell of a lot worse for me than Lois too. She was going back to college in the fall. I had to live in Buckminster. And I had a widowed mother to look after, and a sister who wasn't all there."

The medals pinned to their chest. This was the guy. What was it Alvie Comeau had said? *One that got the medal.*

"Dot!" Mrs. Smees was back in her office and unhappy.

Bas must have heard my heart pounding and misread it. "I'll have her back in a jiffy, Muriel."

"Who was it?" I said.

"Can't be 100 percent positive about a man's identity if you've only seen him from behind. Let's just leave it at that."

"But you recognized him, didn't you?" I knew he did. "How?"

"Get back to work."

"Was he really tall or something? Short? Fat? What?" Then I had an idea. "It was his coat. He was wearing a long coat, like an army coat, wasn't he?"

Bas's face scrunched up in genuine confusion. "I don't know nothing about no coat."

"Were his first two initials E.B.?"

Bas didn't answer, but I could tell I was right.

"Dot!"

"Hold your horses, Muriel. She's coming."

He picked up the tablecloth and wrung the water out of it. The muscles in his arms sprang like plucked wires.

"You better get going before she hauls you out by the scruff of your neck. But a word of advice, Dot. You like your job? Then keep your mouth shut."

Twenty-Three

A TINY BABY.

A pool of blood.

A woman—a girl?—curled up in the back of a car at the side of the road.

A man slipping through the woods behind the clearing, something in his arms.

I sat in the staff cafeteria, staring at my hamburger casserole, picking over everything I'd seen or heard, hoping they'd miraculously congeal into some sort of theory.

The mother had to have known the way to the clearing or had someone take her there who did. It was just too hard to find otherwise.

Everything kept pointing back to someone from the Arms, but that didn't narrow it down too much. By the sound of it, anybody who'd ever worked there had been to the clearing. Even Mrs. Smees, hard as that was to believe.

An employee—a young one, at least—would have known that on Tuesday nights the place would be empty.

Provided the dance at the Boat Club didn't get canceled.

I choked down a forkful of peas.

Is that what happened? The mother went there for privacy but got caught off guard when they kicked everyone out of the club?

Maybe she'd had to hide really fast when she heard people coming. But why wouldn't she have taken the baby with her then? Itty-bitty little thing. Easy enough to carry, even slip into her pocket, by all accounts.

Or had she left the baby there on purpose? Left me there to the elements. Not wanted me. Too tired, too sick, too confused to figure out what else to do with me?

I squished the peas with the back of my fork, their tiny brains exploding through the prongs. What kind of mother would do that? Desert her own flesh and blood. No chance of survival.

But then I realized that's not what had happened. I'd survived. Someone had found me, got me to the Home, made sure I had a life.

Maybe that's what the mother had wanted. She wasn't just leaving me there. She was leaving me there *for* someone. She'd known someone would come and get me. *The baby will be at the tree. Please look after her for me.*

I liked that theory better.

I took a bite of casserole, but it was cold and rubbery now—which was only moderately worse than warm and rubbery—and I pushed it aside. I checked to be sure Ida wasn't looking, then got up and scraped my plate into the garbage can.

That's all I was thinking of—dumping the casserole—but the garbage can was right beside the wall with the photos on it. Every employee, year by year, all the way back to who knows when.

I wasn't sure it would do much good other than letting me put names to faces, but I scanned the wall until I found the summer of '47. The photo was taken outside the boat-house. There were a few old guys, but most of the employees looked like teenagers. Some were sitting on the dock or on upturned boats, legs hanging over the edge. Others were lined up class-picture style, tall ones in the back or crouching in front. The names were written below in neat black letters.

It didn't take me long to find Bas. The sleeves of his uniform were rolled up high on his biceps, and that curl of hair still tumbled over his forehead. He had a cigarette cupped in his hand. Like Sandra said, a bad boy.

I searched the names until I spotted Lois's. Tall pretty girl, but I couldn't confirm how great her legs were. A guy in a sailor's cap was crouched in front of her.

Sandra was there too, three kids over, but with decidedly darker hair than now. She had her arm around the shoulder of another waitress and her thumb up in the air.

I checked the names and figured out the other girl was the infamous Cecily Ingram. When Sandra told the story, I'd pictured a beauty—milky skin, silky hair, nose a perfect little triangle—the classic rich kid. The real Cecily didn't look like anything special. The photographer could have just caught her at a bad angle, I suppose, or maybe rich people can be ordinary too.

Dougie Pratt was stretched out on one of the overturned boats. One knee up, hand dangling off it. Dark tan. Nice enough-looking guy. Smiling to be polite or because he was told to, not because he found anything wildly funny.

Ida was there as well, and we were right—she was pretty cute back then, with her lipstick and her Rosie the Riveter scarf. How old would she have been? Mid-twenties? Hard to tell. Not a whole lot older than Bas. She just seemed to have aged faster.

I could hear her clanging away behind me now. I turned around. She was wiping a table as if she was scraping paint, the dimply raw chicken of her upper arms slapping against her side with every stroke.

"This you in the picture, Ida?" She might know something.

"More than likely. Been here forever." She lined her hand up with the edge of the table and swept cold macaroni into it, not interested enough to look.

"You were a knockout," I said.

Now she threw her cloth over her shoulder, dumped the crumbs into the garbage can and waddled over to take a peek.

"Yup, that's me." She tapped the glass. "My husband said he married me for my figure—so I kept making more of it for him."

"That's not Bas, is it?" I was just chatting until I could figure out how to ease her into the whole Bye-Bye Baby conversation. Didn't want her clamming up on me too.

"Handsome devil, wasn't he?"

"Girls must have loved him."

"Oh, they did, all right. Except the one he wanted, of course. But ain't that always the way." She shook her head and turned to get back to her work.

"Which girl was that?"

She rubbed her hand over her mouth. "What was her name?" Looked at the ceiling. "Oh for heaven's sake. I'm not that old." Turned back to the photo. "Minister's daughter. I'll know her when I see her."

She ran her finger over the picture until she came to Lois. "Not her. Bas went out with this one for a while but only to make the other girl jealous. *Just because she broke your heart, doesn't give you the right to break someone else's.* That's what I told him."

"Which other girl?" Now I was just being nosy.

"She's here somewhere." Ida moved her head as if she was watching a very slow Ping-Pong game. "Little bit of a thing. About your size. Bas was crazy about her from the time he was a young fella. Never understood why. Nice girl and all but nothing much to look at. And you know Bas. Coming home from school every day with a black eye,

and her being little Miss Goody-Goody. Ah. Here she is."
She blew a little dust off the glass. "Lucinda Harvey."

"Lucinda?" My voice caught in my throat. That's what
Miss Cameron had called me.

"I know. *Lucinda*. Can you believe it? But her mother
was like that. Always putting on airs."

"Which one is she again?" I said.

Ida pointed her out. Lucinda was standing at the far end
of the second-last row, even though everyone else that far
back was taller. She had limp hair. Thick glasses. Ida was
right. Nothing much to look at.

"Now what the heck is she wearing?" Ida said, and
we both stepped closer. "Everyone was supposed to be in
uniform."

Only Lucinda's head and the lower part of one arm were
visible. The arm stuck out from the end of the row in kind of
a pretty gesture, as if she'd just given somebody something
or let go of a child's hand. You could see the ruffled edge of
her sleeve.

I noticed a hint of a ruffle at her neck too, and then, just
like that, I knew what she was wearing. It was gray in the
picture, with a darker stripe around the edge, but I bet had
I seen it in color it would have been bright yellow or pink.
Something little kids would like.

Ida figured it out at the same time. "It's that clown
costume," she said. "That's what it is."

A girl in a clown costume. Lucinda was one of the girls
Sandra had thought might be the mother.

"I forgot she did that." Ida was still talking. "Lucinda looked after the kiddies that summer. She came up with this idea of calling herself Loosey Goosey. The little ones loved her. Always doing crafts with them, teaching them about wildlife and flowers. But see what I mean?"

My heart was chugging gallons of extra blood into my brain, preparing me for the shock. This could be her. This could be my mother.

Ida was looking at me.

"Sorry. What?"

"Bas? Going out with a girl who dressed up like a clown? Never would have worked. Mind you, better than who he has now."

"Who's that?"

"Nobody." She slid the rag off her shoulder and began wiping down tables again.

I turned back to the photo, my hand flat against the wall, propping me up. I leaned in closer and peered at her. Small. Medium-brown hair—or dark blond, perhaps. Freckles. Was she my mother?

"What happened to her?" I said.

Ida didn't look up. "Lucinda? Got sick that summer. That kissing disease. What's it called?"

"Mononucleosis." I couldn't stand it anymore. "Ida. You know about Bye-Bye Baby?"

She stopped and put her fist on her hip. "What does that have to do with Lucinda?"

"You don't think she could be the mother?"

"The mother of what? An imaginary baby? Honestly. And anyway, that girl wasn't kissing anyone, let alone…well, you know. Good as gold, Lucinda was. I think she's the only kid other than you who ever brought all her dishes back."

Twenty-Four

"OH, OF COURSE. Lucinda Harvey! Haven't thought about her in years." We were sitting on her verandah again. Miss Cameron seemed delighted when I told her who I thought she was mixing me up with. "So glad you came by to straighten me out. I was worried I was turning into just another dotty old lady."

I laughed, although I was still catching my breath. I didn't care what Ida'd said. As soon as I'd made the connection, I'd run all the way to her place. Top speed. So excited at what I was going to be able to tell Eddie.

"You know, there is a bit of a resemblance, now that you mention it." Miss Cameron eyed me like I was a bowl of fruit she was thinking of painting. "Small-boned. Little chin. Something about the hands. I can see it. You know, I actually rather liked her, poor thing."

"Why poor thing?" I said.

"Miserable life for a young girl. Only child. Her mother died of pleurisy when she was small. Her father was the minister at St. Ninian's." She took a sip of the "thimbleful of sherry" Frieda allowed her once a day. "He was the Right Reverend Archibald Harvey—and about as much fun as that sounds."

"How'd you meet Lucinda?"

"Oh, I'd always known her a bit. St. Ninian's was my church, but I never thought much about her until after the war. As part of his parish duties, her father visited all the vets recovering from their wounds. Isabel Adair—Ward's mother—was a great friend of mine. Reverend Harvey came to see Ward and Len every Sunday afternoon with that poor little girl in tow, bored senseless. Isabel called me up and asked if I'd take her on as a student. Of course I said yes. No one should have had to spend their days with Archibald."

Miss Cameron called out, "Frieda!" in a surprisingly singsong voice. "See if you can find Lucinda Harvey's portfolio in my studio." Then she turned back to me. "I tried to keep a little something from each of my students."

"What happened to her?"

"I taught her for about a year. Then I told Ward—his mother had died by then—that he had to hire her at the Arms. I was better company than Lucinda's father, but I was still an old lady. She needed to be with young people. He got her teaching the children arts and crafts. I understand she was quite good at it."

"I heard she left suddenly."

Miss Cameron looked at me over her glasses. "You make it sound suspicious, as if she'd gone to visit an aunt or something."

She laughed. "You don't know that expression, do you? Used to be when a girl disappeared all of a sudden, people would wink and say she'd 'gone to visit an aunt.' It was code for *pregnant*."

"Do you think that's what happened?"

Miss Cameron put her hand on her chest and gasped. "Lucinda? Hardly. Unless I missed something entirely, in which case I'd be extremely disappointed in myself."

Frieda appeared with the portfolio. "Thank you, darling," Miss Cameron said. "Let's see what we have here."

Miss Cameron put the portfolio on the wicker coffee table and leafed through the papers inside. "'Men seldom make passes at girls who wear glasses.' Now you must know *that* expression. It's one I'm quite sure would have applied to Lucinda. Terrible thick spectacles she had to wear. Distorted her eyes. Made her look like a bookish Chihuahua. But look here. I made her take them off when I sketched her. Rather pretty, wasn't she?"

She handed me a black-and-white drawing of a girl curled up in the very chair I was sitting in. She had her elbow leaning on the armrest, her chin in her hand and not quite a smile on her face.

"Pity it's not in color. Lovely blue eyes she had, as I recall. Almost azure. Maybe that's why you reminded me of her. That and the jawline." She ran her finger along the sketch. I could see it too.

"Was she much of an artist?"

Miss Cameron pursed her lips and shrugged. "I had students with more skill but never more imagination. I'd send other girls out into the woods to find something to draw and they'd come back with mayflowers or daisies or something predictable like that. Lucinda was not predictable. Here's the type of thing she'd come back with."

She pulled another drawing out of the portfolio. It was done in charcoal and kind of smudged, and I could see it was no masterpiece.

"Her perspective's a bit off, and her lines a little cruder than I like, but what a subject. A bird skeleton! Only Lucinda would have thought to do that."

It was her. I was sure of it.

"Where is she now?" I said. She had to be around here somewhere. Lucinda had to be the person leaving me the bones.

"Toronto, I think, but I haven't seen her in years. Once her father died, there wasn't much reason to come back, I'd imagine."

It was almost eight o'clock. Frieda arrived with Miss Cameron's bedtime ration of toast, and that was my cue to leave.

I practically skipped back to the colony. I'd found my mother. Oddly, I wasn't even worried about explaining the whole story to Eddie. I figured he'd be so thrilled, none of the stuff about my being an orphan would matter anymore.

The only question still to answer was, Who was the man at the clearing? His initials were E.B. something. The look on Bas's face had proved I was right about that. I tried to remember what else Bas admitted to seeing—the man, something in his arms, something that made him recognizable, even from behind. I knew the answer was there. I just didn't know what it was.

There was a root that bubbled up from a big tree near the Meat Department. I'd walked around it at least twice a day since I'd arrived at the Arms. This time, I was so lost in my head trying to figure the mystery out that I walked right into it. Smashed my big toe. Pain and pins and needles and embarrassment bolted up my leg and into my face. I bit my lip, hopped around on one foot, then limped back to the cabin, sucking my teeth.

And in my head I heard Bas's voice. *Him limping off through the woods.*

That's what he'd said. And in that instant I knew what he meant.

Twenty-Five

BAS WAS STILL scrubbing when I went back and no happier to see me than the last time.

"What now?" he said, and I realized we used to be friends.

"He limped," I said. "That's how you knew who it was, isn't it?"

Bas pulled a sodden wad of cloth from the sink and checked it for stains.

My hands kept clenching into fists. I had to know—but I couldn't bear to find out.

"You only saw his silhouette, but you recognized him. You could tell by the way he walked," I said. "You knew exactly who it was."

Bas scratched his neck with wet fingers. Water dripped black down the back of his green uniform.

"Anybody around here would have recognized him," I said. "He had a bad leg."

Bas stood up straight, slapped his hands on either side of the sink and stared at the wall. He was so mad or upset that you could almost see heat waves coming off him, like a toaster on high. When he spoke, though, his voice was flat.

"No. The man didn't have a bad leg. He had a good leg." Bas made a noise almost like a laugh. "He was missing the other one."

He turned the tap on full blast. Steam billowed up. "That what you wanted to know, Dot? Happy now?"

Twenty-Six

THERE WAS A note tucked into my door.

Come to the dock as soon as you get this. Really need to talk. Quigley canned the Bye-Bye Baby article. Someone's not happy about us doing it.

Eddie xo

It was the *xo* that killed me.

Eddie was my brother—or at least my half brother.

I checked to make sure the cabin door was locked, pulled the curtains closed and tried to think.

Run.

Run-run-run-run-runaway. That song Sara and I used to listen to. That's what I needed to do. Run away.

I'd been happier before I met Eddie. I'd been happier when I got to choose my parents from newspaper clippings and movie trailers and pictures in Mrs. Welsh's *LIFE* magazine. I'd been happier when I was an orphan.

I pulled my suitcase out from under the bed and threw it open, determined to go that very instant, then stopped short.

That stupid coat.

I took it out, laid it on the floor.

I thought how proud of it I would have been when I was at the Home. Patsy could have been talking about her mother being a model at Eaton's before she got herself pregnant, or Sharon bragging about her cousin winning the Durham County road race, and instead of just nodding or trying to think of something else until they'd finally, mercifully, stopped, I could have jumped in and said, "My dad was a war hero."

And they'd have gone, "Was not," and I'd have said, "Was so. You can even ask Mrs. Hazelton. He lost a leg in the war, and he got a medal for it."

"Right," they'd have said, making a big show of nodding over their shoulders at each other as if I'd just made it all up. So I'd have said, "I'll even show you his coat. His war coat. He lost a button too."

I sat on the floor of the seamstress's cabin, kind of laughing *and* crying at that, because it was true. That person I used to be—that little kid, that desperate love-me, love-me little kid—that's the kind of thing she'd say. He lost a leg *and* a button, as if that made it even more devastating, and I wouldn't realize how ridiculous that was until they all started laughing, and then it would be a few more days before I could laugh at it too.

No use blubbering about it now. I needed to get my wits about me and go.

I took out my money and counted it: sixty-eight dollars and twenty-five cents. That would be more than enough to get me back to Hope, but I didn't want to go there anymore. I wanted to go someplace where no one knew me, where I'd never need to explain anything, where I could just be Dot. An insignificant Dot.

There was a train that came through on Sunday. Maybe it could get me to Toronto or New York. Someplace far like that.

I just had to avoid Eddie until then. But how? If I didn't show up at the dock soon, he'd come looking for me. Nowhere to hide in this little cabin. Too far to walk into town. I'd be afraid to hang out in the woods all by myself until dark.

The same three thoughts did a loop of my brain until I heard noises in the colony. The first of the waitresses were getting off the evening shift.

Glennie, I thought.

French fries.

I decided to take her up on her offer.

Twenty-Seven

WE ALL PILED into Finlay's car—me, Glennie, Janice the redhead and some guy called the Weasel, whose girlfriend worked at the Esquire Diner and could apparently get us free French fries. Glennie made sure I was squeezed up next to Finlay in the front seat.

Finlay drove with one finger on the steering wheel and half a smile on his face, as if he found something moderately funny or himself extraordinarily charming.

Everyone jabbered on about people I didn't know and places I'd never been, and that suited me fine. The gossip and the noise and the Weasel's high-pitched laugh almost kept my mind off Eddie.

With the exception of the black-and-white-checked floor, the Esquire was done entirely in not-quite-matching shades of turquoise. Glennie led us to a booth at the back, and we squeaked in across the vinyl seats. Finlay sat with his legs in a wide, manly V, making the rest of us clamp ours

together like cookies lined up in a tray. He stretched his arm over the top of the booth, leaving a warm damp spot just under his armpit for my head.

The Weasel's girlfriend, Trina—hair backcombed into a haystack, miniature bow tucked in above her bangs—took our orders while the Weasel ran a hand up and down her leg. It took her four times around the table before she got our orders more or less straight. She sauntered off giggling.

"Apologies to the Wease," Glennie said, "but that has got to be the world's worst waitress. Even I'm not that bad."

"Trina's nothing," Janice said. "Dot's way worse than her."

I didn't have time to object—*Who, me? A waitress? What?*—before Janice launched into a comic retelling of how I'd knocked boiling hot coffee all over Mr. Peters.

Glennie loved it. "Did he go utterly mental on you?"

I twitched my neck and shoulders to suggest, *Not really* and just hoped she'd drop it. I suddenly had a lot of sympathy for Mr. Peters. I realized it wouldn't be that difficult to lose your mind.

"Oh, please," Janice said. "You want to see mental?" She tucked her chin in and bugged her eyes out and did a pretty good imitation of his whole *You. Why. You.* thing, then grabbed the Weasel by the neck and shook him.

"He actually throttled you?" Glennie grinned at me.

"No," I said.

"Did he?" She was talking to Janice now, who only let go of the Weasel to answer.

"Okay. No. But you could tell he was dying to. Even now, anytime she walks by, his face goes all white and crazy-man. All very Boston Strangler, if you ask me. I'd watch myself, Dot, if I were you."

Finlay wiggled a comb out of his back pocket and began to smooth the hair on the sides of his head as if he were icing a wedding cake. "I don't know how Adair handles it, looking after that nutcase day in, day out."

"And all the while looking after Gunky too," Janice said.

"Why does he have to look after Gunky?" That was me. A trickle of laughter ran through the group.

"Have you seen him?" Glennie asked.

The Weasel tipped his hand back in front of his face like he was glugging from a bottle.

"It's terrible. Mummy says that before the war he was positively yummy. They all were. Ward, of course, was utterly gorgeous. But Len, if you can believe it, was the best. Apparently, nothing like being a medic for six years to play hell on your looks."

"A medic?" Janice started to laugh. "The guy goes berserk at the sight of blood. How could he be a medic? Remember last year when he went nuts over that prime rib of beef at the Dominion Day buffet?"

Chuckles all around. Glennie, to be fair, said, "If I saw that many boys reduced to hamburger, I'd probably lose my taste for rare meat too."

Trina brought our order. Glennie picked up the French fries that fell on the table and stuffed them into her mouth.

"It's a sin. Almost twenty years since the war ended, and the most eligible bachelor in Buckminster is still a bachelor because he's stuck looking after those two. If you ask me, he's taking this whole true-blue-loyalty thing too far. It's killing him. Or at least his social life."

I watched Glennie talk and laugh and eat. Word would get out about us. A little place like this. I wondered if in the years to come she'd remember me as anything more than the scandal of 1964.

We were past curfew by the time we got back to the resort, so Finlay turned off the engine and glided into the parking lot. Everyone whispered goodbye and headed off in their own directions.

"I'll walk you back," Finlay said.

"I'm okay. It's just over there."

"I know where it is." He smirked as if he'd just said something clever.

"Okay. Fine." I figured I might as well shut up and get it over with. I beetled to the cabin as fast as I could.

"You're hot to trot," he said.

"Long day," I said.

"But the night is short."

"Which is why I'm anxious to get to bed."

We were past the lilac bush now. I could see a note stuck in my door, no doubt from Eddie, no doubt wondering where I was. I stood on the first step so I could slip it into my pocket without Finlay seeing, then turned to say goodbye.

He put his hands on my waist. "Anxious to get to bed, are you?"

I put my palms on his shoulder. "Anxious to get to sleep. So thanks for the ride—"

"I can think of a better way to thank me. You could ask me in."

"But I'm not going to."

He leaned against me. "Sure?"

"Yes." I pushed him away. A button popped off his shirt.

"Just four more to go," he said.

"Leave," I said.

"We're just getting started."

"No. Go."

He shoved me up against the door of the cabin, pushing his fat, French-fry-flavored tongue into my mouth.

I bit down as hard as I could. He swore and jumped back, his hand checking for blood. I unlocked the door, stepped inside and locked it behind me.

He stood outside the cabin, banging at my window, spitting every so often, threatening to ruin me in all sorts of ways I hadn't already managed to do myself.

I stopped listening and started packing. When he finally left and there was enough silence for me to think, I unfolded the note.

What happened? How come you didn't come to the dock? Really need to talk. We've got to decide what we're going to do.

Eddie xo

He'd said *we*.

For a moment I let myself forget everything else and just remembered how nice that used to sound.

Then I tore the note into little pieces and went to bed.

Twenty-Eight

I DIDN'T SLEEP. I was too busy planning my escape or fending off unpleasant thoughts—and even pleasant ones, because they turned into the worst kind and hurt the most.

In the morning I got dressed and stepped outside into the sunlight. I felt like my eyeballs had been marinated in nail-polish remover overnight.

There was another note stuck in my door.

You better get out of here fast. You aren't safe.

I didn't recognize the handwriting—a childish scrawl— but I had a pretty good idea who the note was from. Finlay couldn't scare me. I'd be long gone by the time he got off work.

I got to the housekeeping office at ten to eight. Mrs. Smees said, "You have trouble sleeping last night?" I must have looked bad. "Well, don't think that's an excuse to get nothing done today."

I nodded and sat down at my sewing machine. I set to work, brainlessly patching napkins and hemming tablecloths.

At ten thirty, Mrs. Smees disappeared into the laundry room for a few minutes and came back with a bundle of freshly pressed napkins. "Take these to the gazebo set up near the beach. Tell Mr. Oliphant they're for the head table."

I didn't want to go. I didn't want to run into anyone, but what choice did I have? I went. The lawn between the lodge and the lake had been transformed. There were tables, chairs, tents, giant flower arrangements, all sorts of people buzzing around, but no Mr. Oliphant.

Glennie was in the midst of the hustle, popping buns into her apron pocket, goofing around. Janice was there too, but actually working. I finally spotted Mr. Oliphant struggling with a tent pole at the far side of the crowd. He saw me and his face scrunched up as if something smelled bad. He'd never forgiven me for the coffee incident.

I handed him the napkins and hurried back toward the lodge so I wouldn't run into anyone else. Not fast enough.

"Dot!"

I kept going.

"Dot!" And pounding feet.

I turned around, made my face smile.

"Hey!" Eddie's hair looked like he'd had a windy ride across the lake. "Where were you last night? Didn't you get my note?"

"You left a note?" Weak.

"Really?" Like, *You're kidding me.* Waiting for the joke. "Mr. Quigley called me in to—"

"Could we talk about this some other time? I've got to go. Mrs. Smees..."

"Sure. But don't worry about Muriel. I'll look after her." Laughing now. "There's someone you have to meet."

"I can't."

Taking my hand. "C'mon." Running. "Only take a second." He whistled as if he was calling a cab. A man sitting on a log at the edge of the beach turned, put his cigarette into his mouth and saluted.

"I really don't have time, Eddie."

"Nonsense."

He dragged me down to the beach and the man. "Dad," he said with a big smile, "this is Dot Blythe."

Gunky's face was sunburned, lines and wrinkles engraved in red skin. His shirt could have used a cleaning. He kept his cigarette in his mouth and said, "And here I thought Eddie'd been exaggerating—but you're everything he said you were and an ice-cream sundae too." His words were a bit slurred, but it was the floatiness of his head that did it. He'd been drinking. "Forgive me if I don't get up."

I said, "That's okay" and took a few steps back. "I've got to get going anyway. Nice to meet you, Mr. Nicholson."

"Who's this Mr. Nicholson? My name's Eric—but call me Gunky," he said. "Everyone does."

Eric.

E.

I couldn't even say goodbye. I turned and ran back to the lodge.

Eddie ran after me for a while, calling my name, then stopped. Just stopped. Let me go.

I'd thought that's what I wanted, but it didn't feel like it.

Twenty-Nine

MRS. SMEES LAID into me for taking so long to drop off the napkins. I got back to my mending but had trouble negotiating even the straight seams.

Run away. Run-run-run-run-runaway. That's all I could think.

Twenty minutes later there was a knock at the door, and Eddie bounded in. "Sorry, Muriel, but Mrs. Naylor asked to borrow Dot for a few minutes."

"*Now?* The garden party starts in two hours. I might need her. I've—"

"Can't imagine Mrs. Naylor asking if it wasn't important. Could be something to do with the party. Isn't Ward master of ceremonies?"

She swatted us away. "Okay, okay. Take her. I'll make do."

He handed her a sticky bun. "No. Take a break. I'll have her back in two shakes."

We headed down the hall. "What does she need done?" I said in my most humble-servant type of voice.

Eddie had a sort of blank all-purpose smile on his face. "I'll tell you in a minute."

He led me to the path in the woods, not speaking. I was worried he was going to wait until we were out of sight and then kiss me. I was worried he wasn't going to.

He stopped behind an old pine. He checked to see if anyone was around, then said, "What the hell was that all about?"

"I don't know what you're talking about." I didn't.

"Don't even try, Dot. You know damn well what I'm talking about. Running off like that. You ashamed to be seen with my dad?"

I opened my mouth. I shook my head. That's not what it was about at all.

"You have no right to judge him. You have no idea what he's been through."

"I don't judge him."

He snorted at that. "You know, you had me fooled for a while there. Girl like Glennie or Janice, I'd have expected something like that. It's just the type of people they are. But I honestly thought you were different. Not just another rich kid doing time at the Arms because her parents want her to 'learn the value of a dollar.' You actually work. You've got a brain in your head. You're decent. And then this. Treating him like a piece of garbage."

"I wasn't."

"You were so."

"No. I was just busy. You surprised me. And the big party is…"

He was staring at me, calculating his next move. "Okay. Then come down to the beach and talk to him." He took my hand, started to walk out of the woods.

"I can't. Mrs. Smees." I dug in my heels.

"Yes, you can. She thinks you're at Mrs. Naylor's." He pulled.

I wouldn't move. "What if she sees us?"

"She won't. She never goes to the beach."

"I can't."

"You don't want to be seen with my father. There's no other possible reason."

"No, it's not that."

How was I going to explain this? Admit the truth? I wasn't brave enough for that. Apologize? Go back and see Gunky? Carry on as if I didn't know? I couldn't.

"It's not your father. It's—"

"What?"

"I've met someone else."

Eddie dropped my hand and stepped back. "Who?" He turned up his palms, an entirely different person now. "Who?"

I didn't know anyone. The Weasel? He had a girlfriend. Bas? I couldn't.

"Finlay."

"Finlay Hart? You're not serious."

"I am."

"He's a jerk. You know that, Dot. What could you possibly like about him?"

"None of your business."

"It is so. You owe me that much." Not mad now.

I looked at my fingers. He was right. I did owe him that much. "He's funny." Not really. "Good-looking." At least, some people thought so.

"Good-looking? Dot. I've caught fish that are better-looking than him—and smarter too."

I thought he was trying to make me laugh, but when I looked up, his face was sad.

"I don't understand. I thought this was like, I don't know, a thing. I thought we were serious." He put his hands on my shoulders, and they were warm, and I could feel myself giving in.

I pushed them away. "Yeah, well, me too, but then I realized I was being an idiot. I'm sick of you flirting with everyone who moves."

"Flirting? Me? With who?"

"Janice."

"Janice Petley-Jones?"

"I saw you outside the kitchen that day. Whispering, giggling. Hands all over her."

"What are you talking about? I've seen Janice, like, once this year, and I don't even remember what we were talking about. Filling Oliphant's shoes with gravy. Something stupid like that. A joke. I wasn't flirting. I was just being, I don't know, *me*."

"And were you just being *you* when you gave me Libby's jacket?"

He twitched like a bug had just landed on his eyelid. "What does that have to do with anything? You didn't have one. She left it at my place—"

"Yeah. And what other garments did she leave?"

"I don't know. Who cares? I'm not apologizing for going out with someone before I even met you. You're different. This is special."

"Sure. Special. You pull the same shtick with all the girls. Hidden Bay. The ham sandwiches."

"You've been talking with Glennie."

"Good thing. You weren't going to tell me, were you?"

"Why does that even matter? I didn't know you then. Now I know you. I like you. We do different stuff. Dot. Please. I don't know what's going on."

"Nothing's going on. That's what I'm trying to tell you. We're done."

"This isn't right." He looked at me and kind of smiled like, *C'mon. It's me, Eddie*. "Please. Why are you doing this?"

"Why?" I said. "Why should I go out with a caretaker from some crappy little town when I could go out with a college boy?"

Thirty

"SO WHAT DID she need you for so desperately?"
Mrs. Smees said.

I mumbled something about a silk dress with a torn lining and she said Mrs. Naylor never wore anything other than a cotton housedress, and I said maybe it wasn't hers, could have been a friend's— at which point she huffed and said I should stop stalling and get back to work.

My sewing machine kept saying, *EddieEddieEddieEddie*, and I kept thinking, *SorrySorrySorrySorry*. I had no choice. This had to end.

And now I had to get out of there.

I left for lunch on the stroke of twelve. I needed to see a train schedule. The guy at the front desk didn't have one, so he sent me to the reading room. There were only two other people there, a man snoring over a newspaper, and a lady reading *Chatelaine*.

The schedule was right where it should be, and I was in luck. Sunday was the only day of the week with an evening train. It was heading to Albany, New York. A one-way ticket was eleven dollars and fifty cents.

The clock on the wall said 12:17. I couldn't go back yet. Mrs. Smees would get suspicious. I didn't want to go to the staff cafeteria, for fear of running into Finlay, or to the beach, for fear of running into Eddie.

I flipped through a magazine but couldn't keep up the pretense very long. There was something else I wanted to do. I found the album for 1947 and looked for signs of my mother.

Dances. Weddings. Baptisms. That same picture of the Adair Scholarship party we'd seen in the *Gleaner*, the one with Miss Cameron and Glennie's sparkly mother. I turned the page. A big picture of two men in bathing suits, arms around each other, laughing, a single medal with an extra-long ribbon strung around both their necks.

Headline: *Swimmers Combine Forces to Win Race.*

It wasn't until I read the caption that I realized who they were.

"Gunky" Nicholson and "Ward" Adair were once again crowd favorites at the Annual Dunbrae Swimming Regatta. As they have every year since returning from overseas, the former swimming instructors bound themselves together and competed as one two-legged competitor. Adair lost his right leg in a tank accident in Belgium. Nicholson lost his left leg fighting in northern France. Says Nicholson, "I went over to give Hitler a boot in the hindquarters. I never expected him to keep it!"

I stared at the photo for a long time. Gunky wasn't a tall man. He was almost a head shorter than Mr. Adair. They were tied together around the waist and the legs. Or what was left of their legs.

"Are you all right, dear?" the lady said.

I said yes, but I wasn't. I felt hot, feverish. I turned the page, not sure what this meant.

Boat races. Barbecues. Rose gardens in full bloom. Then July 8. My birthday. My birth day. Nothing out of the ordinary. Nothing of interest to me in July at all.

And then it was August, and a headline jumped out at me. *Lucinda Harvey wins Adair Scholarship.*

I read the article.

In an unprecedented show of generosity, the Adair family has made it possible for two Buckminster students to attend university next year. At the annual July ceremony, Cathleen MacDonnell received a full Adair Scholarship to the University of Western Ontario. Now Lucinda Harvey has won the same honor, to attend Victoria College at the University of Toronto. Edward B. "Ward" Adair explains the unusual move. "Miss Harvey has not only maintained high academic marks throughout her school career but also has an exemplary record of community service. She is a beloved children's caregiver at the Dunbrae Arms and a dedicated volunteer at Buckminster Manor for the Aged. We thought it was only fitting her achievements be recognized."

Ward was short for Edward.

I had to catch my breath.

E.B. Adair.

That wasn't Gunky's coat. It was his.

I read the article again, my heart not a drumbeat any more but a drumroll.

Lucinda volunteered at Buckminster Manor. Alvie wasn't confused. He recognized something about me.

I inspected the photo. Lucinda wasn't smiling the way you'd think a person who'd just won a full scholarship would be smiling, but that's not what got me. What got me were the words written across the plaque she was holding.

It said *Adair Scholarship* in large letters and then, under that, the family motto.

I'd read it wrong before. Not *Loyal on the earth.*

Loyal unto death.

The whole true-blue-loyalty thing.

Thirty-One

IT WAS 12:36. I ran back downstairs and slid through the front door of the laundry room. Bas had his feet up on the table, sandwich on his chest, paperback in his hand.

"This is my lunch break, Dot. Come back at quarter to."

"Just one sec, Bas. One sec, and then I won't bother you again. Please."

He closed his book over his thumb, looked up at me. I didn't wait for him to say yes or no.

"You weren't talking about Gunky." That's all I said.

"No. I wasn't. Why would you think that? You knew the guy's initials were E.B." He made a sound almost like a laugh and opened his book again. "And anyway, Gunky knows what's his and what ain't. He wouldn't do something like that."

I ran back out the staff entrance, onto the back lawn. What had I done?

What was the matter with me? Jumping to conclusions, not thinking things through. It couldn't have been Gunky. He wasn't tall. He wasn't rich enough for cashmere or mustard spoons. All those boys who went to war. Why did I assume he was the only guy to lose a leg?

The place was swarming with people—waitresses, grounds crew, ladies with flowers—all setting up for the garden party. I made my way past the crowd and down to the beach, but I was too late. They weren't there.

I squinted up at the patio. I didn't see them there but wasn't surprised. Gunky didn't look like he was in any shape to be dining at the Arms.

The dock. The boathouse. I scanned the yard. Glennie was sauntering down from the lodge with a tray of glasses.

"You seen Eddie?"

"Yeah, I did." She puckered up her face. "He was awfully foul. What's up with him?"

"Where'd you see him?"

"On the dock. Good hour ago. He and Gunky took off somewhere."

"Where?"

"No idea."

I covered my face in my hands.

"Gee. What's with the dramatics? And by the way, what the heck did you do to Finlay?"

"Nothing he didn't deserve." I ran off. "If you see him, tell him we need to talk."

"I don't think he'll be able to. Something's the matter with his tongue."

"Not Finlay. Eddie. Tell Eddie I need to talk to him. Please, Glennie. Please."

Thirty-Two

IT WAS 12:52 when I got back to the housekeeper's office. A woman was standing at Mrs. Smees's desk, her back to me. The tight white bun and broad behind seemed familiar, but it wasn't until she turned around that I could put a name to them.

"Why, Dot. I was hoping I'd catch you." Mrs. Naylor smiled at me. "I just came to pick up Ward's good suit. He thought he was going to get away with wearing his old one, but I wasn't going to stand for that."

I tried to nod. Mrs. Smees was going through her top drawer, not looking at me. Mrs. Naylor tapped the desk and said, "Well, better be on my way, Muriel." Then to me, "Seen Eddie recently, dear?"

"Yes. No. Not really."

She laughed. "I feel the same way with that boy. He breezes in and out so fast, you're never sure whether he's a mirage or not."

I could feel Mrs. Smees getting angrier and angrier. She knew we'd been lying about the dress.

"Oh, listen," Mrs. Naylor said to me. "We should have a chat sometime about Hope. We probably have a few people in common. You wouldn't know Agnes Hazelton, would you?"

I said no, but she didn't fall for it. As soon as I handed her that spoon, Mrs. Naylor figured out who I was.

"Oh, too bad. Thought you might. She's quite well known in those parts." She smiled, and I couldn't help noticing that she left empty-handed. She clearly hadn't come to get Ward Adair's suit.

I spent the afternoon in a panic, not sure what to do. If I could just find Eddie, I could explain why I'd done what I'd done. How I'd thought he was my brother. How it had seemed like my only option. And in my mind, I saw him putting his arms around me, forgiving me, and we were happy again.

And then it flipped, and instead he was telling me he could never forgive me. It wasn't just him I'd insulted, but his father too. How could I possibly believe Gunky would do something like that? I was as bad as all the rest.

Or maybe Eddie would forgive me but wouldn't want me once he found out I wasn't the rich guy's daughter—at least, not the rich guy's daughter he'd thought I was. I was just a lying, necessitous girl. An orphan.

And anyway, who was I kidding? Ward Adair wasn't going to want me around, that was for sure. I wasn't even a townie. I was lower than that. I had to go.

Times flies when your heart is breaking. It was ten after five when I looked up from my sewing machine to see Mrs. Smees standing in front of me.

"Here's your pay. There's twenty dollars extra in there, in lieu of notice. Thank you for your service. We won't be needing you anymore."

Thirty-Three

I WAS TO pack my bags and vacate the premises as soon as possible. I asked why, but all she'd say was, "Your services are no longer required." She wouldn't even look at me.

Mrs. Smees knew. That's why she was getting rid of me. Mrs. Naylor knew. Lloyd Quigley knew too. Ward Adair must have told him to kill the article. (On top of everything else, had I ruined Eddie's career too?)

I had to catch the nine o'clock bus into town if I was going to make the late train to Albany and oblivion. I got out my suitcase and started throwing stuff in. Just as I was finishing up, I found the three postcards I'd bought to send to Mrs. Hazelton and the girls.

I had other people to send them to now. Funny. It was the first time I'd ever written a letter to real people.

Dear Eddie,

You're right. I'm not who you thought I was. I'm not a college girl from a fancy family. I'm an orphan from the Benevolent Home for Necessitous Girls in Hope. I should have told you that right from the start, but I was worried you wouldn't like me if you knew the truth. Then I found out—or at least I thought I found out—that you were my brother, and by that time I was too much of a coward to say anything except horrible things that I didn't really mean (including that stuff about Finlay being good-looking). I needed to make sure you'd never want to have anything to do with me again, because I was pretty sure if it was left up to me, I

And that was all the room there was on the postcard, even with writing up the sides and along the little white strip on the front where they'd put *Dunbrae Arms—Where Happiness Happens!* and it still wasn't enough to say everything I wanted to say, like how I'd never been as happy in my life as that time we sat in front of the seamstress's cabin and laughed and laughed about a baby disappearing in the woods, and how I'd never been as sad as I was right at this very moment. I tore the postcard into tiny bits and threw them out the window.

I took out another postcard.

Dear Bas,

I'm sorry I couldn't stick around to tell you all about my mystery. Thank you for trying to look after me. You were right. I should have kept my mouth shut.

I hope things get easier for you once peach season is over.
Your friend (I hope),
Dot

I took off my uniform and put the postcard in the pocket. He'd find it when he did the next load.

Then I took out the last postcard.

Dear Mr. Adair,

I understand my birth complicated many people's lives and realize why you couldn't keep me. I don't know what you were thinking when you took me to the orphanage. If it was because you wanted to give me a chance at a good life, you did the right thing. I grew up with lots of friends and was well looked after. I owe you my existence, and for that I'm very grateful. I hope my presence this summer has not been too disruptive.

Yours sincerely,
Dorothy (Dot) Blythe
PS Thank you for looking after Gunky and Len too.

I put the postcard in the pocket of the cashmere coat, then changed into Lorraine's aqua linen suit. It looked a little odd with Glennie's sneakers, but at least they were comfortable. I had a long trip ahead of me.

I looked out my window and made sure no one was around. The party was in full swing now, so the colony was deserted. I left my uniform on my bed and headed out the door with my stuff.

Going down the path through the woods, I thought of my mother. The mousy little minister's daughter with the thick glasses and big imagination. Had she been afraid? Did she want me? Or was she trying to get rid of me?

And was she the one who had left me the bones? I didn't know. I tried to figure out what they meant. What she might have meant by them.

And then decided not to. Thinking about my parents had only ever gotten me in trouble. When I was little, it was why I wasn't listening. When I was older, it was why I'd forget what I was doing. Now it was why I was leaving.

It was almost dark and had started to rain. I made it to the edge of the woods and peeked out. No lights on in the big house, just as I'd hoped.

There was a light on in the little cottage, but the curtains were shut. Eddie told me once that there was always a light on there. Len didn't like the dark.

I tiptoed past the cottage, banged my shin into a metal garden chair, then ran up to the house, cursing under my breath.

I took the coat out of my suitcase. I was just going to leave it on the patio, but after all it had been through, I didn't want it to get wet. I decided to leave it in the kitchen instead. I remembered Eddie feeling along the top of the doorframe for the key. I stretched up as far as I could, but my fingers barely touched the frame.

I heard a noise behind me. I turned around.

Leonard Peters was standing on the patio. Eyes and mouth twitchy. Angry.

"I told you to go. Didn't you see the bones? Didn't you see the note?"

Thirty-Four

"**THEY'RE GOING TO** be back soon."

Mr. Peters grabbed me by the wrist, his hand cold and sticky and tight. "We have to go." He pulled me away from the door. "Now."

I struggled. I kicked. I pushed him away, but I couldn't make myself scream.

"You can't fight. Not this time. We're leaving," he said and dragged me up toward the woods behind the house. I tried to grab the doorknob, the pillar, the flower box—anything in my path—but he pulled until my hands gave way.

He took both of my wrists and brought his face close to mine. "I'll carry you, if I have to. You understand?" I was terrified. He smelled like he was terrified too—or maybe just unwashed. I nodded.

I stood up and he started dragging me again. There'd be no one back in the woods. Not tonight. Everyone was working at the party.

"I'm sorry." I wanted to explain that I hadn't meant to spill the coffee on him, but that's all I could get out.

"You're always saying sorry. Don't talk. Don't say anything." The woods were dark. The leaves were starting to get slippery. I tripped, and my knee slammed into a rock. I thought he was going to get mad at me again, but he helped me up and said, "We can't go by the road because they'll find us. We'll stop for a bit at the clearing, but then we have to keep going."

"Where are you taking me?"

He put his hand over my mouth and waited at the edge of the woods until a car drove past. Then he half-carried me across the resort road.

When we were in the woods on the other side, he took his hand away and put me down. "I'll take you anywhere you want," he said, but it still sounded like a threat. "I'll do better this time. I have money. It was just the blood before."

Why was he talking about blood? I started to shake.

"I should have been able to help you." The words and the voice didn't match. "It was my fault the baby died."

He took a breath, wiped his hand over his mouth. "I'm sorry, Lucinda..."

I blinked, shook my head. *Lucinda?*

He turned and really looked at me for the first time.

"I let you down, Lucinda. Our baby died because of me."

Is that what this was about? It was just a mistake. He was confused.

"I'm not Lucinda, Mr. Peters. I'm Dot."

"Don't say that. They know you're here. I've heard them talking. They're going to get rid of you. They think you want something from me. They think that's why I'm upset, but it's not. I want to do right by you this time, Lucinda." He took my hand and started walking again. "We have to go. They'll be back soon."

"I'm not Lucinda." I wouldn't move my feet.

"I told you. Don't say that. People are always treating me like I'm crazy. You were the only one who didn't. I knew you were Lucinda the moment I saw you. Ward tried to tell me you weren't. So did Clara. But they can't fool me. We can be together now."

I took a step toward him, put my hand on his face. He closed his eyes, let his cheek lean into it.

"Mr. Peters," I said. "Len." I shook his face until he opened his eyes. I wanted him looking at me when I said this. "I'm not Lucinda. You didn't let me down. You're the reason I'm alive. I'm the baby."

❧

I held my father's hand and led him through the woods and across the road and back to the Adairs'. The rain had stopped. Two police cars were pulled up on the lawn, and the lights in the house were all on.

Ward and Gunky were on the patio, ties undone, talking to policemen with notebooks in their hands.

Mrs. Naylor saw us first. She slapped her hands on either side of her face and shouted, "Len!" Ward and Gunky started running toward us. They both had a limp, but Ward's was much more pronounced. It would have been hard to miss.

Eddie was there too, but he held back.

Thirty-Five

20 July 1964

Dear Dot,

I'm sorry this has taken me so long to write. I had quite a shock when Ward called to tell me what had happened. I didn't quite know how to respond.

With an apology? With an excuse? I promised myself I'd avoid those. Instead, I'll start where all good stories start—and I do hope this turns out to be a good story—at the beginning.

My father was the Right Reverend Archibald Harvey. My mother died when I was twelve, so it was just the two of us. He used to take me on his house calls to visit the unwell. That's where I first met Len. He was living in the cabin at the Adairs'. I saw him there with Father after the war, but we rarely spoke.

The fall of '46, when I was seventeen, I started taking art lessons with Miss Cameron, and a whole new world opened up for me. I was freed from my obligations to my father and encouraged *to express my creative side. She'd send me out into the woods for inspiration. Len went there for solitude. We met again.*

I was shy initially. He was a lot older than I was—almost twenty-five—and also not the most approachable person. (I actually hid from him the first time I saw him!) But one day, I found a bird skeleton in the woods. It must have been there for ages, as it had been picked clean. I was looking at it with new eyes—Miss Cameron eyes—enjoying its lines and textures and form. Len saw me.

"What's so interesting?" he said, then apologized for startling me. He knelt down beside me and told me what each of the bones was and speculated about whether they'd come from a starling or a thrush of some type. He'd been a biology major before the war and an amateur ornithologist. We started to talk. There, in the quiet, he was an ordinary man. An interesting, wonderful, ordinary man. Not the bundle of nerves I'd seen pacing at the Adairs'.

After that, every time I went into the woods I hoped I'd meet him. Eventually, I'd run into him enough times to realize he wanted to meet me too.

Of course, we had to keep it secret. There was the age difference, my being a minister's daughter and the fact that I'd been involved in a relationship, albeit an innocent one, with a local boy named Basil Simmonds. Most of all, though, there was Len's mental health. No one would have approved.

I was still going to Miss Cameron's art classes and could meet him on the way home. We just needed some way to make

arrangements. Len figured no one was going to be suspicious of
small bones left in the woods. (Wild animals die too, he used
to say.) We came up with a number of different signals, but I
can only remember two. If he left the bird skull by the sign to
Cameron Lane, it meant he wanted to meet me at the tree near
the clearing. If he left the wing, it meant "Don't go. Danger.
Someone's coming." I don't believe we ever had to use the wing,
but Len wanted to be careful.

And we were—about that, at least. But then one thing led to
another. It only happened once. I thought it was the beginning of
our life together. Len, unfortunately, thought different.

I saw the skull by the sign the next day and raced up to the
tree. Len was there. He apologized. He said he'd acted dishonor-
ably and begged my forgiveness.

I tried to argue with him, but he wouldn't listen. He wasn't
a man anymore, he said. He couldn't look after me. He couldn't
give me the life I deserved. I told him I didn't care about any of
that, but he just kissed me on the forehead and told me it was
over. We could never see each other again.

I was devastated but had to hide that too. I couldn't eat.
I couldn't sleep. It was my last term of school. I wanted to die.

My periods had never been regular. When they stopped,
I just thought it was because I'd gotten so thin. My mother had
died before she could explain the facts of life to me. I didn't
realize I was pregnant until I was a good five months along and
noticed I was getting a tummy.

I was terrified. I didn't know what to do. I just hoped it—
the "it" wasn't a "you" yet—would go away. I got the job in the

Kiddy-Care Center at the Arms and came up with this idea of Loosey Goosey. I wasn't even admitting to myself why I wanted to wear a big hot clown costume all summer. (I'm afraid I've always been pretty good at sticking my head in the sand when I don't like what I see.)

I had no plans for what I was going to do with this baby when it finally came. I had fantasies, of course—I'd arrive at Len's door with my little bundle of joy, and his heart would melt—but even I knew that was unlikely. By then, he'd had another bad spell.

I figured the baby would come sometime in the early fall. I'd be finished at the Arms by then. I'd have some money. I'd go somewhere. That's all I knew.

And then on Tuesday, July 8, just before the parents came for the kids, I fell down the stairs. I was leading everyone in one of my goose chases around the lodge and those silly clown shoes of mine caught on a brick, and I went flying. The kids all thought it was part of the game, so I had to scramble back onto my feet to keep them from flinging themselves down the stairs too. It wasn't until a little boy pointed out the blood on my costume that I realized something was up.

I went into the ladies' room and tried to stop the bleeding with paper towels, but there was too much for that. I couldn't go to the hospital. I was worried someone would tell. Len lived nearby. He was a medic in the war. He'd know what to do.

Even in crisis, I was scheming to see him. I patched myself up and cut through the woods to his cottage. I knocked on his door but got no answer. It wasn't locked, so I went in. I was going to wait for him but was afraid someone might see me. Mrs. Adair had just died, but Ward, Mrs. Naylor or Muriel Smees (the maid I knew from Buckminster) could have shown up at any second.

Len had a number of bird skeletons on his bookshelf. I put the skull from one on a piece of paper on his kitchen table and drew an arrow pointing at it. I didn't know if he'd understand, but I was too afraid to write anything else. It was Tuesday. The resort kids would be at the Boat Club dance. I made my way up to the clearing and waited. I didn't know it yet, but I was in labor.

By the time Len got there, it was dark. I was in so much pain I could barely talk. I can't imagine what the poor man was going through. He'd come back from overseas with a full-blown terror of blood and, obviously, hadn't had to deliver any babies on the battlefield. But he saw me through. We both thought the baby was dead. You were so tiny. He took off his shirt, wrapped you in it and left you there. He carried me back to his cabin. Then he disappeared.

I don't know how much time passed. Next thing I knew, Mrs. Naylor was with me. She stroked my head and said Ward had gone to get the baby. He'd make sure it got a decent burial. I understand now that by the time he got there, kids from the resort had arrived. He heard the commotion when they found you and hid in the bushes until they took off. He had no idea you were alive until he got you home.

Mrs. Naylor had to calm Len down, so Muriel drove me into town. She wasn't much of a driver, but there was no one else to do it. She went off the road, and her husband had to come get us. Dr. Talbot was waiting at the back door of the hospital for me. He stitched me up, then called my father to say I had mononucleosis and would be staying in the hospital until I got my strength back.

The whole incident plunged Len into a terrible place—and for that I'm very sorry. I was young and foolish and too much in love to understand what I was doing.

Ward arranged a scholarship to get me out of Buckminster and, more important, away from Len. I regret he didn't see fit to tell me the baby had lived—but I don't blame him. A naïve mother, an ill father—Ward decided we were both better off not knowing. Mrs. Naylor had lived in Hope, so she knew about the orphanage. She believed they'd look after you well.

I understand they did.

Thanks to Ward, I was able to go to the University of Toronto and further my schooling. I graduated with a Bachelor of Education degree and taught for several years before I met and married a lovely man, Bob Urquhart. We have three little boys—Bobby, Lenny and Adair—and now, at long last, the girl I've always dreamed of.

Mrs. Naylor tells me you're small and pretty. Ward tells me you're smart and brave. (He's amazed you managed to calm Len down enough to get him back to the house.) Muriel tells me you're an excellent seamstress (although prone to daydreaming). Gunky tells me his son's in love with you.

I look forward to falling in love with you too. When do I get to meet you?

Thinking of you,

Your mother, Lucinda

Thirty-Six

EDDIE TOOK ME to the Esquire Diner, but he wouldn't
come in with me, no matter how much I begged.

"No way I'm coming between a mother and her baby,"
he said. "Could be dangerous." Then he kissed me on the
forehead and pushed me through the door.

The waitress said, "She's in the booth at the back."

It was a long walk.

All my life, I'd dreamed about my parents. Turned out
my father wasn't Steve McQueen after all. He wasn't rich.
He wasn't famous. He was just a kind and gentle man who'd
never really come home from the war. The little bit of fight
he had left in him he'd saved for doing right by me. I was
proud of him, even if some days he wasn't sure who I was.

Still, as I walked through the diner, part of me hoped
that my mother would live up to my fantasies, the ones I'd
had when I was a kid. That she'd stand up in her sequined
gown like she'd just stepped out of the pages of *LIFE*

magazine and everyone in the Esquire would lower their cheeseburgers and whisper, "Oh my god, isn't that...?" And I'd have a story to tell and a reason to be and proof, finally, that all those years of waiting and wondering and *thinking of you* had been worth it.

Lucinda stood up as soon as she heard me coming. She wasn't much to look at—small-boned, pale, thick glasses—but she gasped when she saw me and put her hand over her mouth, then her arms around me, and she sobbed real tears into the crook of my neck.

Better than any fantasy.

VICKI GRANT has been called "a superb storyteller" (the Canadian Children's Book Centre) and "one of the funniest writers working today" (*Vancouver Sun*). Before writing for young adults, she was an advertising copywriter, scriptwriter and television producer. She lives in Nova Scotia with her family. For more information, visit www.vickigrant.com.

Uncover more Secrets—
starting with this excerpt from:

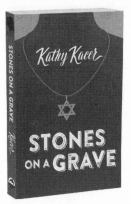

SARA AND PETER stood facing the International Tracing Service building in the middle of Bad Arolsen. It was a solid and impressive-looking brick building encircled by an iron fence. The fence was intimidating enough. The added problem was the security men who stood guard in front, one at the gate and another farther down the walkway, at the front door of the building. The men wore uniforms, though neither Peter nor Sara could identify what they were. German police? Private security? International inspectors? It didn't matter. The men were there to keep visitors like Sara out.

"Why does it look so much like a prison?" Sara asked.

Peter began to explain. "Under Adolf Hitler, the Nazis kept detailed records about their own activities—who they rounded up and killed, where it happened and how. All of that information has been brought here. But I guess this country is not yet ready for the world to see any of it. So they keep it locked up—tightly!"

The two of them continued to stare at the guards.

"What do you think we should do?" Peter finally asked.

Sara had been hatching a plan and decided that now was the time to put it into action. She turned to Peter. "Put your arm around my waist and follow my lead," she directed. Peter was taken aback and looked confused. "Don't ask any questions," she said. "Just follow me."

With only the briefest hesitation, Peter hooked his arm around Sara's waist, and together they began to move toward the iron gate and the first guard. As they drew closer, Sara suddenly slumped against Peter's body and hung her head on his shoulder.

"Halt!" the guard ordered as they approached. The man had a thick neck, and his hands were folded across a uniform that stretched across an overly ample belly. His head was the shape of a full moon, and his jaw jutted out as if someone were pulling on the bottom half of his face.

"Please," Sara gasped. "I need to use the bathroom!" She doubled over, coughing and pretending to retch into her hand.

"*Das ist verboten!*" The guard took a menacing step toward Sara.

She could make out a word that sounded like "forbidden" in what he had just growled at them. "I'm going to throw up," she tried again, grabbing her stomach and contorting her face.

That's when Peter took up the script. "You've got to let us in," he pleaded. "She's going to be sick right here."

As if to prove his point, Sara coughed again, gagging violently. The guard hesitated. Sara coughed louder, lifting her face directly into his.

"Please," Peter begged. "Before it's too late."

At that, the guard stepped back and quickly moved to open the gate. He grabbed his walkie-talkie to signal to his colleague at the front door of the building. Peter and Sara picked up their pace, lurching through the set of gates, up to the front door and past the second, startled security guard who had opened it and stood aside.

"Toilet?" Peter asked.

The guard at the front door pointed down the hallway and stood back, covering his own mouth with a handkerchief as Sara heaved once more.

"That was brilliant," Peter said once they had turned a corner. He held his arm around her waist for a moment longer, until Sara moved away from him and smiled.

"I've lived in an orphanage all my life. You'd be surprised at how many ways there are to get around doing chores or get out of trouble." This had been almost too simple. "You were pretty good yourself," she added.

"Just following your lead," he replied. "But what do we do if we run into another guard?"

Sara took a deep breath. "One obstacle at a time."

The two of them surveyed the signs that dotted the hallway. They were written in German and meant nothing to Sara, but Peter investigated them closely. "There," he said, pointing to one of the arrows. "I think the records of those who were in the DP camps will be in that room." He indicated a door that was just meters from where they stood.

Through the square glass pane, they could see a middle-aged woman seated at a desk in front of a stack of files and papers. Her short dark hair was brushed neatly behind her ears, and her glasses were perched precariously on the end of her nose as she worked over her files.

Once more, Peter turned to Sara. "You're the one who seems to know how to get around these obstacles. Any ideas?"

Sara surveyed the situation and then made a decision. Enough pretending, she thought. It was time to take her chances on being completely honest. She grabbed Peter by the arm, and together they opened the door of the records room and walked inside.

The woman behind the desk looked up, startled, as the two young people entered her office. "*Was machen Sie hier?*" She stood quickly, nearly losing the glasses off her nose. Sara did not need an interpreter to understand that the woman was asking what they were doing there. The rectangular nameplate at the front of her desk was engraved with the name Hedda Kaufmann.

Peter began to respond, but Sara reached out and put her hand on his arm. "Let me," she said and turned to the woman. "Do you speak English?" she asked.

The startled woman nodded. "Yes, of course. Who are you, and how did you get in here? Where are the security guards?" She reached for the telephone on her desk, but Sara placed her hand on top of the woman's.

"Before you call anyone, please let me tell you what this is all about."

She began to talk, explaining that she had lived in an orphanage in Canada up until the day that a fire had burned her home to the ground. She described Mrs. Hazelton and the other six girls, and the journeys that each of them was taking to find out who they were and where they had come from. Finally, she talked about the discovery that her mother was Jewish, had survived a concentration camp and had given birth to her in the Föhrenwald displaced persons camp. The woman remained standing throughout Sara's speech. Her face was expressionless, and Sara had no idea what she was thinking. "I'm staying at the Landhaus Inn in Wolfratshausen—with Frau Klein. I have less than a week to find information about my mother and father—who they were and what happened to them. Please don't turn me away." Sara glanced at the nameplate on the desk. "Frau Kaufmann?" Her voice was pleading. "You're pretty much my last hope."

With that, she stood silently in front of the woman. Seconds passed while Hedda Kaufmann eyed Sara up and down. Sara could almost see the debate going on inside the woman's head while she pondered what Sara had said and decided whether to help. Finally, she gestured toward Peter. "And who is this young man? Is he searching for someone too?"

Sara let out the breath she had been holding. She detected that the harshness had gone out of Frau Kaufmann's voice. "Peter is my friend. He's been helping me."

Frau Kaufmann hesitated. "I shouldn't be doing this..." she said, while Sara stood facing her, hope and expectation written across her face. "All right," the woman finally said, moving out from behind her desk. "Come with me."